W9-BVJ-049

WALT DISNEY

★ ★ ★ ★ ★ ★ ★ ★ ★ ★ ★

Name: Walt Disney
Born: December 5, 1901
Died: December 15, 1966
Position: Movie Maker/Dreamer

Career Highlights:
- Was the first voice of Mickey Mouse
- His first theme park, Disneyland, opened in 1955
- Won the most Oscars ever with twenty-two awards over various categories

Interesting Facts:
- During World War I, he drove a Red Cross ambulance in France.
- His film of *Snow White and the Seven Dwarfs* was the first ever full-length animated film— and won eight Oscars.

WALT DISNEY

HISTORY'S★ ★ALL-STARS
WALT DISNEY

By **Marie Hammontree**
Illustrated by **Frank Irvin**

ALADDIN
New York London Toronto Sydney New Delhi

ALADDIN

An imprint of Simon & Schuster Children's Publishing Division
1230 Avenue of the Americas, New York, NY 10020
This Aladdin edition July 2014
Copyright © 1969 by the Bobbs-Merrill Company, Inc.
Cover illustration copyright © 2014 by Chris Whetzel
Interior illustrations copyright © 1969 by Frank Irvin
All rights reserved, including the right of reproduction in whole or in part in any form.
ALADDIN is a trademark of Simon & Schuster, Inc., and related logo is a registered trademark of Simon & Schuster, Inc.
For information about special discounts for bulk purchases, please contact Simon & Schuster Special Sales at 1-866-506-1949 or business@simonandschuster.com.
Designed by Mike Rosamilia
The text of this book was set in Adobe Caslon Pro.
Manufactured in the United States of America 0614 FFG
2 4 6 8 10 9 7 5 3 1
Library of Congress Control Number 2014933326
ISBN 978-1-4814-1374-9 (pbk)
ISBN 978-1-4814-1378-7 (hc)
ISBN 978-1-4814-1379-4 (eBook)

To Lois Stewart Baumgart

★ ILLUSTRATIONS ★

Numerous smaller illustrations

★ CONTENTS ★

MOVING DAY

FOUR-YEAR-OLD Walt Disney sat on the edge of his seat and swung his legs. For some time he had watched the people in the busy Chicago railroad station. Everybody seemed to be in a hurry. Walt was anxious to get started too.

"Roy," Walt called to his brother, "why are we waiting?"

"We have to wait until they call our train," Roy explained. "Here, come sit down by me. We'll listen for the call together."

Walt climbed up on the seat beside his brother. He was very quiet as he listened. Somebody was calling a train now.

"Detroit. Lansing. Flint. Port Huron. Toronto. Montreal. Train on Track Four. All abooo-a-rd!" The sound echoed up and down the station and back again.

"What do they mean, Roy? All aboo-a-rd!" Walt spoke in a loud voice, just as if he was calling trains. People all around stopped and looked. Then they laughed.

Thirteen-year-old Roy laughed. "They mean anybody who wants to ride on that train had better hurry and get on it. The train will leave in just a few minutes."

"Well, come on!" Walt tugged at his brother's hand. "We don't want to miss it."

"Wait a minute, Walter. That's not our train. That train's going to the wrong place for us.

We're going to Marceline, Missouri."

"Oh!" Walt sat down in his seat again, trying to be patient.

Mr. and Mrs. Disney sat across the aisle from Roy and Walt. They both laughed, but their older sons, Herbert and Raymond, didn't even smile at their small brother. They sat beside their parents and were glum as could be.

Mr. Elias Disney nudged Herbert's foot with his. "I wish you boys had a little of Walter's eagerness. I know you will like our farm at Marceline when you see it."

Seventeen-year-old Herbert shook his head doubtfully. "I'm not sure I will like it, Dad. I'd like to stay in Chicago."

"Me too," said Raymond, who was fifteen. "I'm glad we still have a few days left to be in Chicago. I'm not at all anxious to leave the city for a farm at Marceline."

"Well, those days are going to be busy ones," said Mr. Disney. "We have a lot of packing to do, and we'll have to work fast. We want to join your mother as quickly as possible."

"I hope you'll hurry," said Mrs. Flora Disney. "I'm sure Roy and I will need all the help we can get on the farm."

"We'll work as hard as we can," said Herbert. "But, Mother, you know our hearts won't be in it. We don't want to go."

Mrs. Disney understood. She knew how unhappy her two older sons were. She knew how they hated to leave their friends and their life in the city. She spoke gently. "It's hard to change homes, but a person can never really tell about a place until he's tried it."

"Your mother is right. Someday you will be glad you had a chance to live in the country," Mr. Disney said firmly. "That's exactly why

4

I bought the farm. Why, look at you—soft, no muscles! City life is unhealthy for boys. Sometimes city boys get into bad company, too. Then they get into trouble."

Mrs. Disney could feel another argument coming. Elias was a good father, but he just didn't understand boys. "Now, Elias," she said, "don't be too hard on Herbert and Raymond. It will take time for them to get used to farm life. They will miss Chicago. They will have to make new friends. It's not going to be easy."

Herbert and Raymond didn't say a word. They knew their mother had listened to many arguments between them and their father. They knew she was sorry to leave Chicago too. But Mr. Disney had made up his mind. He had bought the farm, and now they had to move.

"Maybe Roy will like the farm," Herbert spoke at last. He knew he must be more cheerful for his mother's sake. "And there's no doubt about it. Walter will like the farm. Walter will love the animals."

"Ruth doesn't care at all that she is leaving the city," Raymond added, trying to make a joke. "She's sound asleep."

Mrs. Disney hugged the little girl lying in her arms. "Well, our Ruth is only two years old. This has been a big day for her."

"It's a wonder Walter isn't asleep," said Mr. Disney. "He must be tired. He was up long before daylight this morning."

"It surprises me, too. But I expect Walter is too excited to go to sleep. This is a new experience. After all, this will be his first long ride on a train. You know how curious Walter is about everything he sees."

Just then Walt jumped from his seat. "They're calling our train!" he announced.

Indeed they were, and loudly! "Joliet. Streator. Chillicothe. Galesburg. Fort Madison. Shopton. Marceline. Carrollton. Kansas City. Track Two. All abooo-a-rd!"

"All abooo-a-rd!" yelled Walt. "Hurry!"

Once more everybody laughed. This time Herbert and Raymond laughed. They couldn't help themselves. They were excited too.

RAILROAD TALK

The whole Disney family hurried to the train. They got on the train too. Of course not all of them stayed on the train. Mr. Disney, Herbert, and Raymond soon said good-bye. They stayed only long enough to make certain the baggage was properly placed and Mrs. Disney and the children were comfortably settled.

Walt didn't stay settled for long, however. He ran from one window of the train to another.

He didn't want to miss a thing. He especially wanted to see the man in uniform standing by the train steps. "Roy, what's that man down there doing?" Walt called.

"That's the conductor," Roy explained. "He's about to give a signal to start the train."

Walt pressed his nose against the window glass.

The conductor did appear to be giving a signal. He held his right hand high in the air. At the same time he looked at his watch in his left hand. Then, all of a sudden, he gave a loud call. "Booo-a-rd!"

In a few seconds Walt announced, "I think we're moving." He was right. The train picked up speed. It creaked and it squeaked. It rounded a bend in the track. It swayed.

"We're on our way to Missouri!" Walt sang. "We're on our way. We're on our way."

Just then the door of the railroad coach opened. The conductor entered. "Tickets!" he announced. "Have your tickets ready!"

Walt turned to the conductor. "Hello," he announced. "I watched you start the train."

The conductor smiled at the friendly blond boy. He winked at Roy. "I'll bet you can't show me how I did it."

"Oh, yes, I can." Walt stood up. He stretched his right arm above his head as far as he could reach. "Booo-a-rd!" he called.

"Why, that's very good. Maybe you'll become a conductor when you grow up. You already know one of our signals."

"Thank you," said Walt. "I'd like to be a conductor. I like trains."

"Well then, maybe you'd like to help me collect the tickets."

"Oh, Mother, may I?"

Mrs. Disney nodded. Then she warned, "But the conductor is a busy man, Walter. Don't annoy him with too many questions."

Walt followed the conductor happily. By the time he returned to his seat, he and the conductor were good friends.

"We went all the way to the engine," announced Walt. "We watched the mail train grab the mail on the fly, too. They grabbed it with a big hook. They didn't even have to slow down for the station."

"My, you're talking just like a railroader," said Mrs. Disney. "But suppose that's natural. You take after your father. He used to work for the railroad."

"Oh, what kind of railroad work did he do?" asked the conductor.

"He was a grease monkey, whatever that was," Mrs. Disney explained.

Roy started to laugh. So did Walt. Then they caught their mother's eye. They both knew it wouldn't be polite to laugh.

"That's railroad talk," the conductor said. "A grease monkey is a car oiler. Every time a train finishes a trip, the engine is checked from top to bottom. A grease monkey does a thorough job of oiling the engine."

"Grease monkey is an odd name. Where do railroaders get such terms?" asked Roy.

"Oh, the railroads have a lot of terms that outsiders don't understand."

"I know. My husband used to be a snipe, too," said Mrs. Disney. "A snipe was a track laborer. He helped lay a railroad track from Kansas to Denver, Colorado."

"My goodness, that must have been hard work," said the conductor. "I've heard the workers sometimes had to fight off the Indians and the wild animals, too. Did your husband have any trouble like that?"

"I don't believe so. I've never heard him speak of it."

"Indians!" Walt jumped out of his seat. His brown eyes were wide with excitement. "Do you think Indians will attack this train?"

"No, no, young man. This is 1906," said the conductor. "The Indians have all moved to their reservations out West. We don't have to worry about the Indians now."

"Well, sir," Roy said with a grin, "you've disappointed my little brother. He would enjoy nothing better than an Indian attack."

"Don't worry," Mrs. Disney smiled at Walt. "With Walter's imagination, he'll see Indians attacking all the way to Marceline."

Walt grinned back. He knew his mother was teasing.

The family often teased him about his imagination.

The conductor tousled Walt's hair.

"Well, young man, it looks as if you've got a bait can up there on the rack. How would you like me to get it down for you?"

"Bait can?" Walt was puzzled.

"I'll bet that's more railroad talk," said Roy. "By bait can you must mean our lunch basket, don't you?"

"That's right, and it's a good thing you guessed it," said the conductor. "I have a feeling this young fellow wouldn't be happy for very long if he had to fly light."

"If flying light means to miss a meal," said Mrs. Disney, "I am sure he wouldn't. He's always ready to eat."

The conductor handed down the basket. Then he said good-bye.

"Good-bye, and thank you," said Walt.

"Here, Mother, let me hold Ruth for you," Roy offered. He took the little girl.

Soon Mrs. Disney was passing out fried chicken and boiled eggs to her sons. The Disneys were eating happily, and their train was rushing on to their new home in Missouri.

Every so often Walt stopped eating and looked out the window. He still hoped to see an Indian lurking somewhere nearby.

FARM LIFE

EVERYBODY KEPT busy on the farm. The work was never finished. Little Ruth was the only one who had no tasks to perform.

Mr. Disney and the older boys did the plowing and planting. They pruned the trees in their two apple orchards and kept the apples picked. Roy looked after two horses and several cows. He milked the cows morning and night.

Mrs. Disney had her housework to do. She also raised chickens and sold their eggs. In addition, she planted a small garden. This called for weeding whenever she had time.

Herbert, Raymond, and Roy not only helped out with the farm work, but they went to school in Marceline.

Walt expected to go to school when he turned six years old on December 5, 1907. But Mrs. Disney said no. He was too young to make the trip to Marceline each day.

Mrs. Disney had once been a teacher, so she started Walt on his lessons at home. In between lessons Walt took care of the pigs. He couldn't have been happier.

"I'm going to build a pigpen as quickly as I can," Mr. Disney explained. "But until I get the pen finished, Walter, I'll have to depend on you. You must keep the pigs from wandering off. We can't afford to lose any of them."

"Oh, I'll take good care of the pigs," Walt

promised. He did, too. Not a pig strayed from the farm. Walt watched over every pig from the sows down to the tiniest piglet. He carried food for the pigs from morning to night.

There was one pig so tiny that Walt had to give it special care. Mr. Disney said the pig was a runt. Walt called the runt Porky. Walt made sure no other pig pushed Porky aside at the feeding trough.

One morning Mr. Disney said, "Walter, you've certainly made Porky sleek and fat. By now I can hardly tell Porky from the other pigs."

"Neither can I," said Walt. "But Porky knows me. He'll come if I call him. He's smart."

"I'm sure he is. Pigs are among the smartest of farm animals. In the Middle Ages pigs were often used for merrymaking and fun."

"Do you mean people had shows with the pigs?" asked Walt.

"Well, it was something like that. It was considered great sport to put grease on a pig. Then men and boys would chase the pig. They would try to catch hold of it."

"I guess a greased pig would be hard to hold," Walt said. "Sometimes I can hardly hold Porky, and he's not greased."

"I've read, too, that King Louis XIV of France liked pigs. He used to amuse his court by having shows with them. He'd have the pigs dressed up like people."

"Ha, ha! I'll bet that was funny." The more Walt thought about the idea, the funnier it became. Pigs dressed in people's clothing! Walt's imagination went to work. How would Porky look dressed like a person?

He looked about him. There was Ruth playing in the yard. She could spare her hat for a few moments.

Porky was a very clean pig. He wouldn't hurt the hat at all.

"Here, Ruthie, let me have your hat," said Walt. "I'll give it back in a minute." Walt tied the hat on Porky.

"Ha, ha!" laughed Ruth.

"Ha, ha!" laughed Walt.

Porky did not seem to mind wearing the hat. It fitted him very well, and he liked all the attention the children were giving him. He gave a few contented grunts.

"Porky is really laughing," said Walt. "He likes to be dressed up." The children went on playing with the pig and Walt continued to talk. "I wish I could put hats on all the pigs and draw pictures of them," he said.

Walt was pleased to have Ruth approve of his idea. His imagination soared. "Suppose we put a hat on Porky's mother," he said. "Her hat

should be larger and should be decorated with red flowers and green feathers."

In a little while, Porky began to squirm restlessly to get away. The hat was beginning to rub his chin, and he was tired of being held, but Walt didn't understand. His mind was filled with visions of making hats for Porky's mother and all his brothers and sisters.

Then Walt laughed so hard that he forgot to hold on tight. Suddenly Porky was loose, and he headed straight for the muddy pond. Of course he still wore Ruth's hat. But for once Porky didn't answer to his name. He didn't come back, and he was too far ahead for Walt to catch him.

Just then Walt had an idea. Nearby was the old sow who was Porky's mother. Maybe she could overtake Porky. Walt jumped on her back and grabbed her by the ears. He urged the sow toward the pond.

The sow went all right. She wanted to dump this rider off her back. And she did! In a few seconds Walt, the sow, Porky, and the hat were all in the pond. Walt crawled out of the mud. He untied the muddy hat from Porky's head.

"Oh, dear, what will I tell Mother?" Walt wondered. "And what if Dad finds out? He will really be angry."

Then Walt turned around. He had the surprise of his life. His father was running from the orchard. What's more, he was laughing!

"Walter, are you all right? I saw you from the orchard, and I couldn't help laughing. I didn't know you had learned how to ride the hogs. Did you get hurt?"

"Oh, I'm fine, Dad."

But Walt didn't feel fine. Now there was no doubt about it. His father would see the hat, and he'd give Walt a licking.

Then Walt had another surprise. He could hardly believe his ears. Mr. Disney turned back toward the orchard, still chuckling. "Walter, you'd better go in the house and get cleaned up," he said. "You're as muddy as Porky."

Mrs. Disney helped Walt wipe the mud from his face. She brought him clean clothes. All the time Walt wondered. Why hadn't his father mentioned the hat? Hadn't he seen it?

"I'm not surprised. I expect your father was busy looking at you," Mrs. Disney said. "Why, you're mud from head to toe."

Then she scolded Walt a little. She said he was wrong to borrow Ruth's hat, even though he felt certain no harm would come to it. But she said she thought she could make Ruth another hat. She didn't say a word about telling his father. Walt decided she must be the nicest mother any boy ever had.

Many times afterward when company stopped at the farm, Mr. Disney would say proudly, "Come out to the barn lot. I want Walter to show you how he rides the hogs."

Walt was glad to put on a show for his father. He enjoyed riding the hogs, even though he always ended up in the mud. He never again tried to put clothes on Porky or any of the other farm animals. But he did imagine, sometimes, how they would look dressed up.

WALT'S MILKING LESSON

One evening Roy said to Walt, "Come with me, Walter. It's about time you learned to help with the milking."

Walt was happy to go with his brother. He had been interested in the cows for some time. Until now, however, he had always been warned, "Stay away from the cows. You're too young. You might get stepped on."

Walt was pleased that at last he could meet the cows on closer terms. "What do we do first?" he asked on the way to the big red barn.

"Well, tonight I think you had better just watch," Roy told him.

"Oh, all right, but I'm big enough to help."

"Of course you are. Don't fret. You'll have a chance to do plenty of milking. But first I have to teach you how to go about it."

Walt watched carefully as Roy got the milking stool. Then Roy placed a pail under the cow's udder. He braced his head against her side and began. His hands moved steadily and rapidly. There was a rhythmic splash in the pail.

Walt soon found he was not the only one watching. Six of the farm cats were by his side. They rubbed his legs with their bodies. They purred and arched their backs.

"Ha, ha," Walt laughed. "I guess the cats want to learn to milk the cows too."

"No, they're here for another reason," said Roy. "Stand back! Now watch!"

Walt moved back, but the cats didn't move. They seemed to be waiting for something. Suddenly it came! A stream of milk shot toward the cats. Then another and another. Roy's quick hands aimed at first one cat and then the other. But Roy was no faster than the cats. Each cat was ready for its turn. Each cat held its mouth open to catch the stream of milk.

Walt giggled. He jumped up and down with excitement. "Oh, Roy, let me try it."

"I don't know. You haven't watched how it's done long enough. I don't think I had better let you do any milking tonight."

"Roy, please let me try," Walt begged. "I can do it. I know I can."

"Very well. Come here."

Roy placed his little brother in front of him. Then he took Walt's hands in his and put them on the cow. He showed Walt how to milk with even, sure movements. "Now, don't move too fast. And don't be jerky in your movements," he warned. "The cow will not like it if you do. She might even stop giving milk."

Roy and Walt finished milking the first cow. Everything had gone very well. Then Roy said, "Here, you try milking this cow by yourself. She's a gentle one."

"Fine," Walt agreed. "And this time I'm going to feed the cats. I want them to stand around me. That's half the fun of milking."

"Well, I suppose it will be all right. You seem to learn fast."

Walt was careful to give each cat its turn. A few times he missed his mark. But the cats didn't mind a little milk on their fur and whiskers. They'd get it off when they washed up at the end of the meal.

At last the brothers headed toward the house with their pails of milk. "You're doing splendid, kid," Roy said. "I'm glad you're so handy. Very soon Dad's going to need all the help that we can give him."

"Why, what do you mean, Roy?"

"Well, I'm afraid Herbert and Raymond won't be here much longer. They're making plans to go back to Chicago."

"Now, why do they want to do that?"

"You know they never wanted to leave Chicago. I'm sure you've heard Dad and the boys argue about staying on the farm."

"Of course, but I've never understood it. I like the farm, don't you?"

"Yes, I like it."

"I like the animals," Walt said. Then he added emphatically, "I like milking, too."

"I can see you do," Roy said as he put down the pails. "I can also see that the Disney farm is going to have a lot of fat cats."

Walt grinned. He was being teased again, but he didn't care. He did like the farm. He liked everything about it.

BUDDING ARTIST

ONE MORNING Mr. Disney came home from Marceline. He had a bucket of tar in his wagon. He unloaded the tar and placed it near the back door. Then he laid a brush by the bucket.

"I've bought some tar to fix the leak in our roof," Mr. Disney explained to his wife. "Herbert will help me with it when he gets home from school. We can get it done tonight." After that Mr. Disney went off to work in the fields.

Anything new on the farm caught Walt's attention at once. So it was no wonder Walt soon spotted the strange bucket. Of course he had to find out what was in it.

Walt lifted the lid and peered at the thick black liquid. Then he carefully tested it with a finger. "Hmm! Paint!'" said Walt. He picked up the brush lying by the bucket. "I guess Dad's getting ready to paint the house."

Walt thought about this for a while. Surely there could be no harm if he helped. Why not start the painting right now? He stood for a while with the brush in his hand. He looked at the green siding of the house and wondered where he ought to begin.

"I know," Walt said to himself. "I'll begin by painting a picture of Porky."

It wasn't long until Porky's picture took shape. There was Porky's snout. There were his fat sides, his four short legs, and his curly tail. Walt stood back and looked at the painting. He

liked it. He bet Porky would also like it.

But there was somebody who didn't like the painting. It was Mr. Disney. He was just coming in from the fields. "Walter, what on earth are you doing with the tar?" Mr. Disney shouted. He started to run.

"I'm starting to paint the house," Walt explained. "But first I thought I would paint a picture of Porky."

"That's not paint, Walter. That's tar. It's to fix the leak in the roof."

"Oh, oh!" Walt still liked the picture.

"I don't know how I'll ever get that tar off the house," Mr. Disney continued sternly. "But I do know one thing."

"What's that?"

"I'm going to teach a certain boy a lesson. I'm going to teach this boy not to meddle in something that is none of his business. Do you know who the boy is?"

"Yes, Dad."

"Very well, then. March to the woodshed."

Walt marched. He'd been licked before. He

knew what was coming, and he could bear it. But there was something that hurt more than the licking. Mr. Disney hadn't said a word in praise of Porky's picture.

AUNT MAGGIE

Walt loved to meet the train at the railroad station in Marceline. When his Aunt Maggie arrived on the train, he enjoyed it even more. She was a favorite of Walt's.

Aunt Maggie was married to Mr. Disney's brother, Robert. She was always interested in the things Walt liked. She almost always brought him a very special present.

Now Aunt Maggie had come again. Mr. Disney, Roy, and Walt helped her into the buggy for the trip to the farm. "Tell me, Walter, do you still like to draw pictures?" she asked.

"Oh, yes," said Walt. "But sometimes I can't

find any paper. Then I can't draw."

"Why, what do you mean, Walter?" asked Aunt Maggie. "Won't they give you any paper?"

"He means," laughed Roy, "that the rest of us have to keep our schoolbooks well hidden. Walter has drawn pictures all over them. He will draw pictures on anything he can find, especially when he doesn't have any paper."

"He certainly does. And there isn't much I can do to protect the house from his pictures," Mr. Disney grumbled.

"Why, what are you talking about, Elias?"

"Well, just a few days ago Walter got into a bucket of tar I had bought to fix the roof. He painted a pig on the side of the house."

"Oh, no!" Aunt Maggie giggled.

"It's no laughing matter, Maggie. I haven't yet been able to get the tar off the house."

"Well, I can see I've brought the right present

for Walter. Now he won't bother your school books or the house anymore."

During this discussion Walt's face had grown red, but now he beamed. "Oh, Aunt Maggie, what is it? What did you bring me?"

"You'll see. It's the kind of gift that a young artist needs."

"Maggie, I think you're wrong to encourage Walter to draw. Drawing is all right when it's done for fun. But don't want any boy of mine growing up to be an artist."

"Fiddlesticks, Elias! If a boy has talent, he should have a chance to prove it."

"Now, Maggie, you know as well as I do that most artists end up starving to death."

"Well, right now Walter is a long way from starving to death. He's only seven years old. If he wants to draw, I'm going to see that he has a chance to do it."

After that, the trip home seemed endless to Walt. Then, to make matters worse, Aunt Maggie had to have a long chat with Mrs. Disney. Walt wondered if she would ever get to her unpacking. He did want to see his gift.

Of course it wouldn't be polite to mention the gift. He'd just have to wait. Anyway, now it was time to go after the cows.

Walt hoped Aunt Maggie would have the gift unpacked when he got back from the milking.

Walt's mind was full of thoughts about the gift as he rounded up the cows. He was still thinking about it when he reached the barn. Roy waited with the milking pails.

"Roy, what do you think the gift is that Aunt Maggie has brought me?"

"Well, why don't you go and find out? I saw her unpacking as I left the house."

"But you need me to help with the milking, don't you, Roy?"

"Not tonight, kid. You just go back to the house and see about your gift."

"Thank you, Roy."

Walt fairly flew to the house and into the kitchen. Aunt Maggie was setting the table for supper. Walt saw at once that there was a package at his place. Aunt Maggie smiled at him. "Go ahead, Walter. Open it."

Nobody had to tell Walt twice to open that package. He tore off the paper. Then he could scarcely believe what he saw. There were a real artist's drawing tablet and a real artist's pencil. He touched them softly.

"Oh, Aunt Maggie!" Tears came to the boy's eyes. He gave his aunt a big hug.

"You couldn't have given Walter anything that would have made him happier," explained

Mrs. Disney. "Why, I'll bet tonight he will take that tablet to bed with him."

"I will," declared Walt. "How glad I am! Now I can draw pictures whenever I like."

WALT'S FIRST ART SALE

Aunt Maggie had long since returned to her home in Kansas City. Walt's drawing tablet was by now well filled with sketches.

Today Walt sat under one of the weeping willow trees in the Disney front yard. He had his drawing tablet. He was waiting for Dr. Sherwood to come by and take him for a ride.

The country doctor and Walt had been very good friends for a long time. But now Walt seldom had a chance to visit with the doctor. Herbert and Raymond had followed their plans. They were no longer living on the farm. They had returned to Chicago. Now Roy and

Walt had to do all the extra farm tasks. The boys were busy all day long. They had little time to play.

But at noon today Roy had come to the dinner table with exciting news. "Walter, I met Dr. Sherwood out by the road this morning. He asked about you. He invited you to come for a ride with him this afternoon."

"I would like that, Roy," Walt said gravely. "But what about the work?"

"Don't worry about the work. I can handle it for one afternoon. You've been working very hard. You've helped me a lot. You deserve an afternoon of fun."

"Thanks, Roy."

"The doctor said he would stop at the front gate about half past two. He also asked that you bring your drawing tablet."

"I wonder why he asked that," said Walt.

"Maybe he wants you to draw a picture for him," Roy suggested.

Roy was right. Dr. Sherwood said he had thought about it for some time. He would like Walt to draw a picture of his horse Rupert.

"If I hold Rupert still, do you think you can do the drawing, Walter?"

Did he! Walt was delighted. Never before had anybody asked for a picture. He would do his very best indeed.

"I think I'll do a picture from the front," Walt decided. "Now, hold still, Rupert."

But this posing for his picture was strange to Rupert. He bucked. He pranced. He reared and then he danced sideways.

Walt danced sideways too. Then he danced back. He had to keep looking at Rupert from the front. He was determined to get the picture Dr. Sherwood wanted.

"Maybe we'd better try another day," suggested the doctor. "Maybe some other time Rupert won't be so restless."

"Oh, no," said Walt. "I'll get it. Just hold on to Rupert a little longer, please." At last Walt finished the picture of Rupert and showed it to the doctor.

"Why, Walter, that's splendid. Now you must put your name in the corner. All artists put their names on their pictures."

"Should I write 'Walter Elias Disney'? That's my whole name."

"That's for you to decide," Dr. Sherwood told him. "But you should always sign your pictures the same way. Then your signature will become your trademark."

"All right," said Walt. "I'll print my name. I'll print it as 'Walter Disney.'"

"That's a good idea," said the doctor. "Now I

have the first Walter Disney picture ever sold. I'm going to take good care of this."

"Sold?" asked Walt.

"Why, of course. A good artist always gets paid for his work. Is a nickel all right?"

All right? Walt was so excited he could hardly wait to get home. Dad didn't think much of artists. Well, now maybe he'd think an artist in the family wasn't so bad.

"Splendid, Walter, splendid," said Mr. Disney, as Walt showed his father the nickel. "You should get a little bank so you can start to save your money."

Walt frowned. He had thought about what he would do with his nickel. The artist's tablet Aunt Maggie had given him was almost full. He had drawn pictures on both sides of the paper. His plans didn't include putting that nickel into a bank.

That night Walt spoke to Roy about his problem. An artist had to have supplies if he was going to keep in business.

Roy agreed that this was true. "Very well, kid. The next time we go to Marceline, we'll stop and get some more paper."

HARD TIMES COME TO THE DISNEYS

IT WAS December 5, 1910. It was Walt's ninth birthday, but he didn't expect anybody to celebrate. There were too many more important things that had to be done.

This had been a hard year for all the farmers around Marceline. Their crops had been good, but the buyers had been few. Now most of the farmers had little money for food. They had none at all to celebrate birthdays.

Things were even worse for the Disneys. Mr. Disney had been ill with diphtheria. The illness had left him weak and tired, but he wouldn't give up the farm.

With Herbert and Raymond in Chicago, Mr. Disney had only Roy and Walt to help him with the farm work. They did their best, but there was no doubt about it. There was too much work on the farm for one man and two boys.

It was rare now that any of the Disneys had an egg for breakfast. Every egg that Mrs. Disney's chickens could lay had to be sold. It was the same way with the butter that Mrs. Disney churned from the milk.

"It won't hurt any of us to go without butter for a while," Mr. Disney explained. "I don't want to hear any grumbling about it." Nobody grumbled, but they wished they could. Bread without butter was not very tasty.

By supper time on December 5, nobody had

even said, "Happy Birthday." Walt guessed it was just as well. They all felt bad because they were poor. Not being able to celebrate a birthday might make them feel even worse.

"Walter," Mrs. Disney called a short time later. "Come here a minute."

Walt hurried to the stove where his mother was stirring gravy. "What is it, Mother? Do you need some more wood?"

"No, thank you, Walter. There's plenty of wood." Suddenly she whispered. "I've buttered some bread for your birthday. But don't tell your father. Tonight just turn the bread over and eat it upside down."

Walt grinned. "Oh, I will, Mother." Then he thought, *Mother does remember after all. But what a funny way to celebrate my birthday.*

"There will also be some bread and butter for Roy and Ruth. Remind them, when you have a chance, to eat their bread upside down."

"Oh, I will, Mother."

There was even more excitement to follow. When the supper was almost finished, Mrs. Disncy said, "Sit still, everybody." Then she brought out a cake. "Walter, this is your father's birthday present. He told me a few days ago, 'We must save out enough eggs and butter for a birthday cake for Walter.'"

"Why, thank you, Dad."

"I've got a little present too," said Roy. He handed Walt a package. Walt opened it quickly. There was Roy's old penknife shined up like a million dollars.

"Roy, I can't take your penknife."

"Keep it, kid. I only wish I could have bought you a new one."

"I've got something too," said Ruth. She gave Walt an envelope. In it were several pieces of blank paper. "I've saved them for a long time. They're for you to use for your drawings."

Walt hugged her. "Thanks, Ruth."

"Here's something else for you," said his mother. She handed Walt a pair of warm wool mittens she had knit.

"Why, I didn't even expect a birthday cake, let alone all these presents," Walt cried. "This is a wonderful birthday."

"Here is one more present," said Roy. "It came in the mail today from Chicago."

"It's from Herbert and Raymond," added Ruth.

Walt tore off the wrappings. "Look! It's a book! It's *Treasure Island*!"

"Elias," said Mrs. Disney, "do you feel able to play a tune on your violin? That would make this a real party."

"Why, yes, Flora, I do."

"Oh boy!" said Walt. "I'll get your violin, Dad."

It was late that night when the Disneys went to bed. But Walt wasn't sleepy. The sound of his father's violin rang in his ears. He kept thinking, "It's nice when our family has some fun together. I wish Dad was not so stern all the time. We could have fun more often."

DR. SHERWOOD GIVES SOME ADVICE

Elias Disney was a proud man. He was a stubborn man too. His health was getting no better, but he refused to leave the farm.

Dr. Sherwood came every day to see Mr. Disney, and every day they argued. At last the doctor gave up. He turned to Mrs. Disney. "Flora, maybe you can talk some sense into Elias. Half of what's wrong with him is worry. He is worried about this farm, but he won't admit it."

"That's true. There is too much work on this farm for one man and two boys."

"Then why don't you sell out and go to the city? Elias can find work there."

"I'd go gladly. But Elias thinks that boys should be raised in the country. That's why we left Chicago and came to the farm."

"Oh, that's poppycock, Flora. You know it and I know it. Elias knows it too. But he's too stubborn to admit he's wrong."

"Well, I'm sure Roy and Walter will do all right in the city. So will Herbert and Raymond. Both of them now have jobs in Chicago. They like it there, and they're doing fine."

"Of course they are. Your boys are all good, healthy boys. It's Elias I'm worried about. He may die if we don't persuade him to leave this farm and take life easier."

"I believe he has begun to think about leaving.

Just the other day he asked me what I thought of going to Kansas City. He said he'd heard of a paper route there that he could manage. I told him I'd like it."

"That would be a splendid idea. The work would be easy. It would give Elias a chance to regain his health. Try to persuade him to go, Flora, before it's too late."

Mrs. Disney smiled. "I'll do my best. I've lived with Elias for over twenty years. I think I can manage him."

FARM FOR SALE

Mrs. Disney managed very well. In a few days Mr. Disney called Roy and Walt to his side for a talk. He explained that they were going to sell the farm. He said they would auction off the animals and farm equipment first. He had made some signs to tell people about the auction. Now he wanted the boys to put up the signs where people could see them.

Roy glanced outside and shivered. So did Walt. The snow had piled up several inches. It was as cold as the North Pole. But they were obedient boys. Roy went out to hitch up the horse. Walt put on his warmest clothes and his new mittens.

"Wait a minute, Walter," said Mrs. Disney. "I'm heating some bricks in the oven. We'll put them on the floor of the buggy. They will keep your feet from getting so cold."

"I'll get an old blanket," said Walt. "That will help too." Mrs. Disney helped Walt to the buggy with the bricks and the blanket. Then she tucked the boys in.

"Hurry! It's too cold for you to stay out very long," she warned.

"Don't worry. We'll be home as fast as we can," said Walt.

"Giddap," Roy called to the horse. Roy stopped the horse at the nearest telephone pole. "Which of us will put up the first sign?"

"I'll do the first one," said Walt. He jumped out of the buggy and waded through the snow. He tacked up the sign. Then he stepped back to read it. He wanted to be sure he hadn't put it upside down.

AUCTION
Tuesday, January 10
10 AM
ELIAS DISNEY FARM

ALL FARM EQUIPMENT AND STOCK WILL BE SOLD

Walt brushed away a tear with his coat sleeve as he climbed back into the buggy. He hoped Roy wouldn't notice. But Roy did notice. "What's the matter, kid?"

"Oh, I don't know. I guess it's the cold."

"Maybe you're sorry to be leaving the farm."

"Well, yes," Walt admitted. "I've been happy here. Haven't you, Roy?"

"Of course I have," Roy answered. "But you'll like Kansas City, too."

"Kansas City? Is that where we're going?"

"That's right. And there will be all kinds of new things to see and do there."

Walt smiled. He was always curious about new places. "When will we leave?"

"Not so fast. I think Dad plans for us to finish school this year in Marceline."

"Then we're off to Kansas City?"

"Yes, after that, we'll go to Kansas City."

"I guess I'll like it," said Walt.

WALT BECOMES A NEWSBOY

R-R-R-R-R-RING! ROY awoke with a start. Blasted old alarm clock! How he wished it had never been invented! Well, now that he was awake, he'd better get out of bed. It was best not to lie there, even for a minute. If he did, he would go right back to sleep. He turned on the light. He saw that Walt was still sleeping. Roy shook him gently. "Come on, kid. It's 3:30. Time to get up!"

Walt opened one eye, then the other. "What's the matter, Roy?"

"Hit the floor, kid. Don't go back to sleep.

Remember where you are? This is Kansas City, not Marceline. We've got a paper route to deliver, and it's time to start."

"Oh! Oh!" Walt threw back the covers. He hopped out of bed and began to dress.

Roy kept an eye on his brother. He knew what would happen. Walt would sit down to tie his shoelaces. Then his head would begin to nod. He'd go to sleep again.

"Roy! Walter!" Mr. Disney called. "The papers are here." Walt jumped. He finished tying his shoelaces.

"We're coming!" Roy answered.

"Better put on your slickers," Mr. Disney warned. "Wear your boots, too. It's very cold, and there's a storm brewing."

"Shucks! That means extra problems this morning." Roy opened the closet door and began to search for their boots.

Walt pulled on his slicker. "We'll have to be careful that the papers don't get wet."

"We'll have to anchor each paper too. You know how the customers fuss if the wind blows their papers away."

"I know. And Dad gets awfully angry if a customer complains."

At last Roy found their boots. Roy and Walt hurried downstairs. Other boys had begun to arrive for their papers.

"Hi, Dan!"

"Hello, Roy."

"What do you say, Bill?"

"Hi, Walter."

"Hi, Jack."

Mr. Disney's paper route was a large one. He had two thousand customers. He needed several boys to help. In the morning there was the *Kansas City Morning Times* to deliver. After school there was the *Kansas City Evening Star.* On Sunday there was the *Sunday Star.*

Mr. Disney paid $3.00 a week to each of the other boys to deliver his papers, but he didn't pay Roy and Walt. He explained, "I clothe and feed you. That's your pay."

Walt thought about this as he hurried into the darkness with his papers. He wished he could earn some money for himself. He needed art paper and pencils for his drawings. On Sunday afternoon he would like to have money to go to a show as other boys did.

Lightning flashed. Thunder rumbled. The wind blew, and big drops of rain began to fall. Then the big drops changed to a downpour.

Now there was no time to think about extra money. It was all Walt could do to keep his papers dry. He stopped on a customer's porch to catch his breath. While he waited he tried to remember. Had he missed any houses as he hurried through the storm? Any customer that he missed would be sure to call his father. Then Mr. Disney would be waiting when Walt arrived home. He would give Walt a paper. Walt would have to turn around and make the long trip back.

"It's not always my fault either," Walt grumbled to himself. Many a stormy day Mr. Disney had given Walt a scolding. Then he'd given him a second paper to deliver.

Walt always knocked on the door with the second paper. Several times the customer had opened the door, and the first paper had fallen to the customer's feet. It had fallen from between the door and the storm door. That was exactly where Mr. Disney told Walt to place the papers when it snowed or it rained.

"Oh, I didn't think to look there," the customer had said. "I just looked out through the window and didn't see the paper on the porch."

Walt thought about this. His anger grew as he waded through the rain. He was wet and miserable. He was very tired by the time he reached an apartment house. This was his last stop. It would be nice to be inside for a while. He yawned. The

soft carpet on the stairs looked inviting. "I guess nobody will care if I lie down on this landing. I can rest for five minutes before I deliver my other papers. There will be plenty of time."

Walt rested all right. Suddenly he awoke. It was daylight. The sun was shining. The storm was over. "Oh, my!" Walt jumped up. "Where did I leave off with my papers?"

Walt dashed to the top floor. He checked every customer in the apartment house again. Then he ran all the way home. "I suppose there will be no time for breakfast. I'll probably be late for school, and the teacher will be angry," Walt worried. "Ugh! Kansas City! I wish I were back living on the farm."

EXTRA MONEY

No boy in Kansas City worked harder than Walt Disney. He delivered morning papers.

He delivered afternoon papers. He delivered Sunday papers. In between deliveries he went to school. On Saturdays he collected from his customers as well as delivered papers.

Walt's afternoon paper route took him past a drug store. Walt helped out when the druggist needed medicine delivered. Sometimes a delivery could be worked in with his paper route. He made ten cents for each delivery.

A candy store near Walt's school needed a boy to sweep out. Walt got the job. He worked here on his noon recess from school.

One day Walt had another idea. He spoke to his father. "Dad, I'd like to earn a little extra money for myself."

"Yes, I suppose you would," his father said. "What do you have in mind?"

"Well, I've learned there's one corner downtown that doesn't have a newsboy. After breakfast I could sell newspapers on that corner. I'm sure I could sell all my papers and still get to school on time."

"That's a fine idea, Walter. But you must be extra careful not to miss any customers on your route. They come first. You'll have to go back to them if they complain."

"I understand."

"How many papers do you think you can sell?"

"I could start with fifty."

"Very well. I'll order fifty extra papers for tomorrow morning."

The next morning Walt caught a streetcar to his downtown corner. "Paper! Paper!" he yelled. "Get your morning paper!" People liked the new newsboy. In no time at all Walt had sold his fifty newspapers.

The papers cost two cents, but several

customers told Walt he could keep the change from a nickel. "Thank you," Walt said. He gave every customer a big smile. Then he caught another streetcar to take him to school.

There was only one hitch in Walt's plans. When he got home from school, Mr. Disney said, "That money you earned this morning, Walter, I'll keep it for you. Otherwise something may happen to it."

"Well, I had some things that I wanted to do with it, Dad."

"Of course. I know. You wanted to spend it on something foolish. I'll keep it. Later you'll be glad that I did." Walt's hopes fell. That night he told Roy what had happened.

"I know Dad means well," Roy answered. "But it's like Mother has always told us. Dad just doesn't understand boys."

"Well, I'm not going to let him find out

about my delivery job with the drug store, or my candy store job at noon."

"Of course not. And don't worry. I'll look around for some other odd jobs we can do. We'll find some way to earn some money for ourselves in spite of everything."

ARTIST OR ACTOR?

THERE WAS to be a carnival near the Disney home in Kansas City. Walt read the poster announcing the date. Then he ran home to tell the news. His eyes sparkled with excitement.

"They'll have a Ferris wheel and a merry-go-round," Walt announced.

"I've heard there is going to be a balloon ascension," said Roy.

"They will have dart games and shooting galleries and cotton candy."

"They are bound to have hot dogs for sale."

"It sounds like fun," said Mrs. Disney. "You boys must be sure to go."

"We're going."

"It's all right to go to the carnival and look around," said Mr. Disney. "But don't waste your money. Most of the things you spend money for there aren't worth a cent."

"Oh, now, Elias, it won't hurt if they spend a little money," protested Mrs. Disney.

"Well, it's a good thing I've got Walter's money in a safe place. Otherwise he might throw it away on such foolishness."

Walt's heart sank. All afternoon he had been working up courage to ask for some of his newspaper earnings to spend at the carnival. Now he knew it would be hopeless to ask.

"It's not fair," Walt said to Roy later. "It's my money. I earned it."

"Don't worry," Roy whispered. "I have a job

lined up. We'll earn some money. We'll have fun at the carnival, too."

"What's the job, Roy?"

"Well, you know Bill Barnes, the undertaker."

"Of course. He lives on my paper route."

"He needs somebody next Saturday to wash his hearse," Roy said in a low voice. "The job is ours if we can be ready by noon."

"I'll be ready. I'll start early on my newspaper collections."

"Good," Roy answered. "I'll tell Mr. Barnes we'll take the job."

At twelve noon on Saturday, Walt was ready. So was Roy. Mr. Barnes backed the hearse into the street. Roy got a bucket of water and a whisk broom. Then he turned to Walt. "Which would you rather do, the inside or the outside?"

"Oh, it doesn't matter. I guess I'll take the inside," said Walt.

"Very well. Here's the whisk broom. I don't mind telling you that I'm glad you prefer to clean the inside."

"Why, what's the matter, Roy?"

"Oh, I don't know. I think I'd find it sort of spooky in there."

The hearse was a long narrow vehicle painted black. It had long plate-glass windows on either side. Draped at each window were gloomy black curtains, which were closed.

Walt climbed through the door at the back. He closed the door. He brushed up the dust for a few minutes.

Then he stopped to think. "I guess I must be the only live person that has ever been in here," Walt decided.

It was a little spooky. Walt giggled. "I wish

somebody would see me. They'd think I was a dead person come to life."

Walt pulled back the curtains and looked out the windows. He hoped to find some passerby so that he could try out his new idea. Sure enough, a lady was coming down the street.

Walt quickly stretched himself out flat. He waited until he thought the lady was near the window of the hearse. Then he sat up stiffly. The lady looked up. She shrieked and ran.

"Ha! Ha!" Walt doubled up with laughter.

Roy pecked on the door. "Walter, what are you doing in there?"

"I'm pretending I'm a dead person come to life," said Walt. "Now be quiet, Roy. I see another lady coming. Let's see what she will do."

Walt lay back down again. Then he pulled himself up slowly. This time he moaned a little for extra effect.

The lady stopped. She stared. Then she ran to Roy.

"Young man, young man," she gasped. "There's somebody in there who's alive."

By this time Roy was laughing. "It's all right, lady. It's just my kid brother. He's supposed to be cleaning the hearse, but I'm afraid he's playing. He's got a big imagination."

"Hmph!" The lady stalked off.

Finally Roy came to the back of the hearse.

"Walter, I think you've played enough," he said. "Come on out and help me wash this hearse."

"Oh, all right, Roy," Walt answered, laughing. "But I was having such fun."

"Well, there'll be no fun at the carnival if we don't get this job done."

"You're right. And I don't want to miss the carnival. I'll be right out."

A few months later Walt came home from school with some more news. He could hardly wait to tell it. "On February 12 our school will celebrate Abraham Lincoln's birthday. Guess who's going to be Abraham Lincoln!"

"I can't imagine," said Mrs. Disney with a twinkle in her eye. "Who is it?"

"Me!" Walt said proudly. "And I want to dress up to look just like President Lincoln."

"With that blond hair you don't look much like Abraham Lincoln."

"That's true. But I can take a pencil and draw some lines on my face."

"Well, I'll try to find something to darken your hair," Mrs. Disney said.

"Walter, think it's an honor that the teacher chose you for this part," said Mr. Disney. "You must do your very best."

"I will, Dad."

"I have some crepe hair you can use for a beard," said Roy. He ran to get it.

"I used to wear this coat to church in Chicago," said Mr. Disney, producing a long frock coat. "I haven't had it on in years. Flora, could you cut it down for Walter? It might help him look a little more like Mr. Lincoln."

"Why, Elias, that's a splendid idea. Of course I can cut it down."

"Thanks, Dad. I'd like that," said Walt.

"Then I believe only one other thing is needed," said Roy. "That's a tall black hat. Where do you suppose we can get one?"

"Can't we make one out of cardboard?" Walt asked. "We could cut it out and then blacken it with stove polish."

"Of course. We can make it just to fit."

"I'm sure we can," said Walt. "Now if I can

only find somebody to listen while I practice the Gettysburg Address."

"I can do that," Ruth offered.

"You've forgotten one thing," said Mr. Disney.

"And it's the little details that will make your role a success, Walter."

"What have we left out?"

"A mole for your face. Mr. Lincoln had a mole. Do you remember?"

"That's right. He did. Well, I'm sure I can make a mole," said Walt.

All the Disneys worked to help Walt. At last February 12 arrived. Walt was very serious about his role as Abraham Lincoln. He wanted everything to be perfect. This was a special program and the parents were invited.

"I'll be there," said Mrs. Disney. "I wouldn't miss it for anything."

"I plan to come," said Mr. Disney.

They kept their promises. They sat as proud as peacocks when the teacher announced, "Walter Disney will now deliver Abraham Lincoln's 'Gettysburg Address.'"

Walt walked slowly to the center of the room. He was very dignified. His makeup was just right. So was his costume. He tried to imitate Mr. Lincoln. He spoke solemnly.

"'Four score and seven years ago our fathers brought forth on this continent, a new nation, conceived in Liberty, and dedicated to the proposition that all men are created equal.'"

Under her breath Mrs. Disney repeated every word with Walt. She did hope he wouldn't forget. At the end of the address she sighed with relief.

Walt had been letter perfect.

"Wonderful!" said one of the mothers.

"That boy's a born actor," said another.

"The children were very impressed," said the school principal. "I hope Walter will repeat this program for our celebration every year for as long as he's in school."

"Of course he will," Mr. and Mrs. Disney spoke together proudly.

"Walter has talent," said the teacher. "There's no doubt he can be an actor."

Walter heard this. He talked it over with his mother as soon as he could. "I thought I wanted to be an artist. Now I don't know. Do you think I ought to be an actor?"

"Walter, you know your father wouldn't want an actor in the family," Mrs. Disney said.

"Well, I don't think he wants an artist. And I can't be a newsboy all my life."

"No, I suppose not. But let's carry things on like they are for a while. Let's not worry about it yet."

★
A GIFT FROM ROY

THERE WAS one thing Walt wanted more than anything else. It was a pair of high leather boots with a buckle at the top. Almost every boy in school had a pair.

Walt thought about asking his father for some of his newspaper earnings. Then he gave up the idea. Mr. Disney would no doubt say that it was foolish and a waste of money to buy the boots.

Walt tried saving the money from his other odd jobs, but the saving was slow. "It's no use,"

Walt decided. "I'll be an old man before save enough money for the boots."

There was one hope left, however. Christmas was coming. Walt decided to drop some hints. Maybe somebody in the family would buy the boots for a Christmas present.

Walt followed his plan. He never missed a chance to speak of the boots. But Mrs. Disney said nothing. Mr. Disney said nothing. Neither did Roy. Walt was puzzled.

There was little money in the Disney home to buy presents for fun. Everything had to be useful.

Well, those boots were useful! If they were not useful, he'd like to know what was.

One wintry Sunday morning Walt came home from delivering his papers. He was covered with snow. His shoes were wet. His socks were wet. So were his feet. Mrs. Disney helped him to take off his coat and shoes.

"Hurry up to your room and put on some dry clothes," she said. "Then I'll make you some hot chocolate to warm you up."

Walt started up the stairs. After a few steps he stopped and called, "A pair of leather boots would be very useful in the snow. I don't think my feet would get wet in them."

Roy grinned. Mrs. Disney smiled. And Ruth laughed right out loud. "Shh!" Roy warned. "Walter might hear you and ask questions."

Mrs. Disney lowered her voice to a whisper. "How much money have you saved, Roy? Is it enough to buy the boots?"

"It's almost enough. I'm sure there will be enough in a few more days."

"Good! Walter will be disappointed if he doesn't get those boots for Christmas."

"Walter works hard for an eleven-year-old.

He works harder than many men."

"You're right. He has no toys. He wouldn't have time to play with them if he did."

"I've never spoken of it before. But one morning something made me very sad."

"Why, Roy, what was that?"

"A boy on Walter's paper route had left his toy train on the porch. I saw Walter look at it and pick it up. He played with it for a few minutes. Then he put it back as he found it and went on to deliver his papers."

"Walter never complains. He never speaks of the things that other boys have."

"Of course he doesn't," Roy said. "That's the reason I'm so determined. Walter must have the boots that he wants."

"Roy, I'm proud of you for being so unselfish. There must be several things you would like to buy for yourself with that money."

Christmas had come and gone. Walt had his new boots. He wore them everywhere he went. "Are you sure you don't sleep in your boots?" his mother teased him one morning.

Walt grinned. "No, I take them off at night, but there is one thing that worries me."

"What's that?"

"I hope my feet don't grow too fast. I want to wear my boots for a long, long time."

There was still snow on the ground. There were also big chunks of ice. But now Walt walked in snow and ice without a care. He hadn't had wet feet since Christmas.

Tonight he walked toward home. He had finished his afternoon paper route. His day's work was done. For a little while he could take his time and do as he pleased. He walked slowly. He kicked at the ice as he walked. It was fun to break big chunks of ice from the street.

Then a dreadful thing happened. Walt kicked at one chunk of ice. But this time he couldn't pull his right foot away. What was worse, there was a terrible pain in his foot. Each time he pulled, the pain became worse.

"Help! Help!" Walt called.

A streetcar went by, but it didn't stop. Walt could see people only a block away, but he guessed they couldn't hear his cries. They didn't come to see what was the matter.

"Help!" Walt cried again. "I'm stuck!"

Still nobody came. Walt began to worry. It was growing dark. What if he had to stay there all night? At last Walt saw a delivery wagon drawing near.

"Help! Please help!" he called loudly.

The driver pulled to a halt. "What's the matter, boy?"

"I'm stuck."

The driver took one look and knew he'd better work fast. He saw blood oozing from Walt's boot into the snow. He quickly got a pickaxe from his wagon and chopped the ice loose. But Walt's foot still wouldn't budge.

"There's a doctor's office down the street. I'll ask him for help." In a few minutes the delivery man came running with the doctor. The doctor saw at once what the trouble was.

"There's a nail frozen in the ice. It has punctured your boot and pierced your foot."

By this time a crowd had collected. "Oh, my!" they cried.

The doctor made ready to pull out the nail. "I'm sorry, son," he said to Walt. "I haven't a thing to give you to stop the pain. So just hold on while I get your foot loose."

"I'll do my best."

The delivery man offered the doctor a pair of pliers. "Thank you. Now if you and this other gentleman will just hold the boy's leg while I pull! Ready now."

Walt gritted his teeth. At last the nail was out. Then the doctor took Walt to his office. Walt felt a little better until he heard the news. "I'll have to cut this boot away from your foot," said the doctor. "We can't pull it off. You have a bad injury. We don't want to make it worse."

"I suppose not," Walt said bravely.

For two weeks Walt couldn't deliver papers. Neither could he go to school. But little by little his sore foot grew better. After a while it healed as good as new.

One day Walt asked his mother to show him the boots. Sadly Mrs. Disney brought them. "I'm afraid the one boot is no use now, Walter. You can see it can't be fixed."

"I can see. I guess I would look pretty funny hopping around with only one boot."

Walt did his best to smile. Mrs. Disney put her arms around him and hugged him. She had tears in her eyes. She knew how much it hurt Walt to give up his boots.

"I'm glad he doesn't cry or whine," she thought. "He meets his disappointments with courage."

★

COMIC PICTURES

WALT STILL found time to keep up with his drawing. How he did it was a mystery. He even managed to attend classes at the Kansas City Art Institute on Saturdays.

When he wasn't working, going to school, or attending art classes, Walt practiced drawing at home. He drew dozens of pictures. He liked to draw cartoons better than anything else.

Drawing a cartoon was not easy. First, Walt chose a subject. Then he drew a picture of the subject. But he didn't draw the subject exactly as it looked. He picked out something about the subject to emphasize.

If it was a good cartoon, it would look like the subject. But it would also be a comic picture because of the things that had been emphasized. People would recognize the subject, and they would laugh at the exaggerations.

Walt had been drawing cartoons ever since he could read. Whenever he looked at a newspaper, he looked at the cartoons first. He would study each cartoon. He would try to find out what made it funny. Then he would get out his sketchbook and draw pictures like it. Sometimes he drew several before he was satisfied.

Mr. Disney said Walt's cartoons were pretty good. Mrs. Disney said they were excellent. Walt liked to hear this praise, but he never stopped practicing. He was more critical of his own work than they were.

One day Walt came home carrying a magazine.

"Look, Mother! Look at this ad. It says I can learn to draw cartoons by mail."

"That's what they call a correspondence course, Walter," Mrs. Disney explained.

"Do you think it would cost a lot of money for me to take this course?"

"Well, your father will have to decide about the cost. If he thinks we can afford it, he will let you take the course, I'm sure."

"Dad usually says no."

"He always says he wants his children to have a good education."

"I know, but he may think this is a waste of money. He may say it's foolishness. He often says that when I ask for something."

"No, no, I'm sure he won't this time. He's proud of your cartoons. He's especially proud of those you draw about the capitalist and the laboring man."

"Of course he is. That's his favorite subject. The first cartoons I ever drew were copied from that newspaper Dad takes."

"Do you mean the paper called *The Appeal to Reason*?" Mrs. Disney asked.

"That's the one."

"I remember. You used to look at those cartoons by the hour. You were only a little tyke and could barely read."

"I still like to look at them."

"Your father likes the way you draw the capitalist so big and fat."

"That's because the capitalist is rich and has so much to eat."

"Tell me. Why do you always put a square paper hat on the laboring man?"

"Oh, that's because the laboring man is poor.

That's the only kind of hat he can afford. The artists in Dad's newspaper do it that way, so I've learned to do it, too."

"Well, I think your father will be pleased that you want to take this cartoon course. I'll speak to him tonight."

A BUSINESS DEAL

Mr. Disney agreed to allow Walt to take the cartoon course. So Walt wasted no time. He sent for the lessons at once.

"I hope the lessons come soon," Walt told his mother. "I'm anxious to get started."

When the lessons did arrive, Walt carried them with him everywhere. He practiced drawing cartoons in every spare moment.

One day Walt was in Tony's Barber Shop waiting to get his hair cut. As usual, he had his drawing pad. He looked about for something to

draw. Then he sketched while he waited.

He worked so hard that he forgot where he was. He didn't notice the other customers looking over his shoulder. The first thing Walt knew, there was a loud burst of laughter.

"Say, Tony, come here," said one of the customers. "Look at your picture."

"Ha, ha! That's Tony, all right," said another.

"That's just the way he swings his razor when he's shaving us."

"And look at the size of the razor! This kid knows Tony. By golly, the razor looks just that big, too, when Tony's shaving you. You know how Tony swings it as he talks."

"I like the title the kid's given the picture," said the first customer. "'The Closest Shave in Town' is the right title."

"It's true, too. Tony does give you a close shave for your money."

"I think the kid means Tony also gives you another kind of close shave. Don't you, son?" Walt grinned and nodded.

"Ha, ha! That's true. Why, just the other day I had a narrow escape."

"I know. I saw Tony that time. He was excited and forgot to watch where he swung the razor as he talked. I thought for a moment he was going to cut your throat."

By this time Tony had walked over to look at the picture. He began to laugh. "Say, like this. I'd like to hang it in the shop. Where'd you learn to draw, kid?"

"I learned at school," Walt explained. "Now I'm taking a cartoon course by mail. That's what this drawing is. It's a cartoon."

"I'd like to buy it," said Tony. "It would dress up the shop. How much would you charge to let me have this picture?"

"Why, I don't know." Walt was confused. "I never sold a cartoon."

"I'll give you twenty-five cents for it. Better still, if you'll bring me a new cartoon as good as this one every week, I'll pay you twenty-five cents a week."

"That's a good idea, Tony," said one of the customers. "You can put up these cartoons for your customers and their friends to see. It will bring you business."

"I should say it will. After people hear about them, they will come in, just to look at the cartoons. Then maybe they'll get shaves and haircuts while they're here."

Walt beamed. "It's a deal, Tony. You pay me twenty-five cents a cartoon, and I'll bring you a new one every week."

Walt's head was in the clouds for the rest of the day. Why, he hadn't even tried, and he had sold his first cartoon! He forgot about wanting to be an actor. There was no doubt now what he wanted to be. He wanted to be a cartoonist.

SCHOOL PROBLEMS

WALT STILL missed his life on the farm. He missed the farm animals. He longed for a pet. Several times Walt had found stray dogs in Kansas City. Each time he found a dog he lured it home, fed it, and shut it up in the backyard.

"When I come home tonight, we'll have a good romp," Walt would promise. But something strange happened every time. When Walt came home in the evening, the dog would be gone. Walt would never see it again.

This morning Walt had found another dog.

It was only a mongrel, but Walt thought it was handsome. Now at school Walt was supposed to be working on his arithmetic lesson. Instead he was thinking about his dog.

Walt thought about a name for his dog. He thought of the things they could do together. He thought how nice it would be to have the dog along when he delivered papers. He thought of the tricks he would teach his dog.

Best of all, his dog could sleep on the corner of his bed. Roy was no longer at home. Roy had graduated from high school and had gone away to work. Walt had been lonely ever since. Now this dog, Walt thought, would be a nice companion to snuggle up to. The two of them would have much fun together.

Suddenly Walt jumped. "Walter! Walter Disney!" Walt looked around.

"Walter," the teacher said sternly, "are you

daydreaming again?" Walt shook his head.

"Well, then, please go to the blackboard. It's your turn to work the next problem."

My, that was a close call. Walt knew he had narrowly missed being in trouble. This teacher was always fussing at him about something. Just the other day she had scolded him for going to sleep in class.

"Well," Walt thought, "she doesn't realize that I get up at three thirty in the morning to deliver papers. I'll bet she'd be sleepy too, if she had to do that."

As soon as school was out, Walt hurried home to see his dog. He listened for a welcoming bark, but there was none. What's more, there was no dog in sight. Walt searched every corner of the backyard and looked in the street.

Just then Mrs. Disney came to the door. "Your dog got away, Walter."

"Oh!" Walt's face dropped.

"It's just as well, Walter. You know your father would never let you keep it."

"I suppose not," Walt sighed.

Mrs. Disney's heart ached for Walt. She knew how much he loved animals. She knew that a pet would help his loneliness for Roy. But Mr. Disney had said many times, "A city is no place for pets. Besides, we have all we can do to feed ourselves. We can't take on a dog."

Walt knew that what his father said was true. Without Roy's help, the Disneys found it hard to make ends meet.

ANOTHER PET

Walt still mourned the loss of his dog. He was very lonely. But he didn't give up. He kept his eyes open for a new pet. Just a few mornings later he found it.

It was a baby mouse. It was half frozen in the cold October morning. Walt had just headed up a customer's walk to deliver a paper. He saw something moving in the snow.

Walt stopped to look. Then he spied the mouse. "Say, little fellow, what are you doing out here? Something is liable to get you."

Walt had to laugh. The mouse reared up like a prizefighter. It began to spar with its front feet. "Well, I'll have to admit you're a game little guy. But you don't have to worry anymore. You'll be safe with me."

Walt picked up the mouse. He was careful not to let it bite him. The mouse was trembling. Walt put it in his pocket.

"You need a friend, and I need a pet," said Walt. "Surely we Disneys can afford to feed a mouse even if we can't afford a dog."

Walt hurried on as fast as he could. He'd try

to get his papers delivered a little early. Then he'd have time left to play with his mouse. But he had no such luck!

Walt had hurried too fast. He missed a customer. Mr. Disney was waiting when Walt returned home. Walt had to take another paper and go right back again. After that things went from bad to worse.

There was no time for breakfast. Walt barely made it on time to his downtown paper corner. Then a storm came up. Walt was almost late for school. It wasn't until arithmetic class that Walt remembered the mouse.

By this time the baby mouse had had a nap. It had awakened warm and comfortable. Next thing on the program was breakfast. The mouse began to explore Walt's pocket. Then it found a way out. The first thing Walt knew, his pet was sitting on his desk.

Walt reached out carefully. He wanted to get the mouse back into his pocket before the teacher saw it. All would have been well if the mouse hadn't begun to spar again.

Boys seated near Walt watched with interest. Some began to giggle. This drew the attention of the girls. Of course, the girl nearest Walt had to be afraid. "E-eek!" she screamed.

Then trouble broke loose. The mouse ran. Girls climbed on their desks. All of them began to scream. Walt went after his mouse, and the other boys followed Walt. They wanted to help him capture the mouse.

At last the tiny mouse was caught. Walt held it in his hand. "It's shaking," he said. "It's frightened half to death."

"Well, what about us?" cried the girls. "We're frightened too."

"Walter Disney, what am I going to do with

you?" asked the teacher. "One day you go to sleep in class. Another day you draw pictures when you should be working. And now you bring a mouse to class."

"It's only a little mouse," said Walt. "I forgot I had it in my pocket. Honestly, I didn't bring it to school on purpose."

"Well, you can't stay in school with that mouse. You've caused enough commotion with it now. Take it outside and turn it loose."

"But it's only a baby," Walt said. "It needs somebody to look after it."

"Walter!"

"Yes, ma'am, I'll go."

But Walt didn't go willingly. On the way he grumbled, "It looks as if I can't even have a mouse for a pet."

★

FUN WITH MAGIC

ONE SATURDAY afternoon Walt sat in a darkened theater in Kansas City. Mrs. Disney and Ruth were there too. All three of them held their breath. So did the rest of the crowd. Any minute the great magician would appear. Everybody wondered what to expect.

They were not long in finding out. Walt grabbed his mother's arm. "Oh, look!" he cried. "Look at that."

The magician had just walked onto the stage. Quicker than a wink he tossed his gloves into the air. Just as quickly those gloves turned into two doves.

After that everybody sat spellbound. Rabbits were pulled out of hats. A red handkerchief changed to green.

Coins were plucked from the air. They were picked out of hats. One appeared on the head of a bald-headed man near the stage.

"Ha, ha!" the crowd laughed and clapped.

Suddenly the magician had a deck of cards in his hands. He shuffled the cards. At the same time he called for somebody from the audience to come to the stage. He said he would need help with the next trick.

Walt looked at his mother. Mrs. Disney looked at Walt. She knew her son. He'd like nothing better than to be up there with that magician. "It's all right, Walter. Go ahead," she whispered to her son.

Walt never wasted time. He rose from his seat at once and headed for the stage.

"Splendid!" said the magician. "Here's a young man who is willing to help. Just for that, I'll teach him to be a magician."

Walt beamed. This was better than anything in his wildest dreams. The magician handed Walt the deck of cards. "Give them a good shuffle, son. Then give me about half the deck—either half. It doesn't matter."

Walt shuffled the cards and handed the magician half of them. The magician turned his back. "I won't look, but please do as I say. Cut your cards once. Then look at the top card. Hold it up so everybody in the front row can get a good look at it too."

Walt did exactly as he was told. He held up the ace of diamonds.

"Has everybody seen the card?"

"We've seen it."

"Very good. Now, young man, put the card back on top of the deck."

Walt followed instructions. What Walt didn't know was that the magician was also working with his half of the cards. He turned the bottom card face up. And he had turned the second card from the top face up. It was on these two cards that the trick depended.

Now the magician turned around. He placed his cards on top of Walt's cards. "Very well," he said. "You look like a pretty smart boy to me, so I'm going to make this as difficult as possible. Put both hands behind your back, please, and listen to my directions."

"Oh, poor Walter! What is that magician trying to do?" Ruth wondered.

"Shh!" said Mrs. Disney.

Now the magician told Walt to slide off the top card and push it into the middle of the deck. "Have you done that?" he asked.

"Yes, sir."

"Good. I'm sure you remember the card you showed to the audience?"

"Yes, sir."

"Fine. Now think hard about that card. At the same time turn the top card of the deck over so it is face up. Then push it, face up, into the middle of the deck."

Of course, since Walt held the cards behind his back for the trick, he didn't know the card was already face up. Neither did the audience. Walt was really turning the card over just like the rest of the cards.

The magician continued. "Now, young man, bring the deck of cards out so everyone can see it. Then run through the cards until you come to your face-up card."

"Here's the face-up card," said Walt.

"Very well. Now we'll find out whether you're a real magician. It depends on where you pushed that face-up card into the deck. It should be next to the card you showed our audience. By the way, what was that card?"

"The ace of diamonds," Walt said.

The magician reached over quickly. He pulled out the card lying under the face-up card. He proudly held up the ace of diamonds.

"What did I tell you? He's a smart lad. He's a real magician. Come on, everybody, let's give this young magician a hand."

The magician clapped. The audience clapped. Walt felt foolish. He'd been fooled, and he didn't like the idea. He knew he hadn't done any magic, but the magician had. He'd like to know how the magician did that trick.

WALT'S MAGIC TRICKS

Walt talked about the magician for days. So did Mrs. Disney and Ruth. They couldn't decide which trick they liked best.

"I think I liked the end of the show," said

Ruth. "Wasn't it splendid when the magician shot off his magic pistol and the girl with an American flag appeared on the stage!"

Mrs. Disney said, "I still wonder how he managed to pour a gallon of tea from a quart bottle. I can't figure it out."

Walt agreed. "I wonder about that too. But the card tricks puzzle me. Imagine squeezing a deck of cards until it gets smaller and smaller! I wish could do that."

"He squeezed the cards until they finally vanished altogether," said Ruth.

"But in a few minutes they came back again, full size," said Mrs. Disney.

"Did you know you can buy magic tricks?" asked Walt. "Here in this magazine is an advertisement from a place that sells them."

"What sort of tricks do they have?"

"Oh, all kinds," Walt said. "I've saved a little

money. I think I'll order some card tricks and a plate-lifter."

"Whose plate do you want to lift?"

"I don't know—anybody's I guess. It sounds like fun. That's why I want it."

"Well, go ahead and get the tricks," said his mother. "Let's have some fun."

Walt sent his order at once. It was only a short time later when the magic tricks came in the mail. "I'd like to see how that plate-lifter works," said Mrs. Disney.

"May I try it on your pots and pans?"

"Of course."

Mrs. Disney and Ruth roared with laughter. So did Walt. The pots and pans would tip first one way and then the other. "They look like they're dancing," said Walt.

"They do, indeed. Walter, you must show me how to work it. I want to try it tonight."

"You want to try it?"

"Yes, I want to try it on your father. He's always so serious. I'd like to see if I can make him laugh tonight."

"That's a fine idea," Walt agreed. "It will do him good. I'll show you."

Walt rigged up the little flat bulb under his father's plate. Then he ran the tube to his mother's seat.

The moment food was on the table for supper, the fun began.

The first thing Mrs. Disney served was vegetable soup. As soon as Mr. Disney lifted a spoonful to his mouth, she squeezed the bulb. Her husband's plate dipped to one side. Then it dipped to the other side.

Walt almost choked with laughter. So did Ruth. But they dared not laugh out loud. Their father hadn't noticed a thing. Again and again

Mrs. Disney rocked her husband's plate. But the effort was all wasted. He didn't see it, and of course he didn't laugh.

However, he did notice something was wrong. "Flora, what on earth is the matter with you?" Mr. Disney asked. "What's so funny? I've never seen you act so silly."

Mrs. Disney chuckled. "I may be coming down with something, Elias," she said. "I'm going into the other room and lie down."

"Humph!" said Mr. Disney. "I never heard of an illness that makes people laugh."

Walt and Ruth finished serving supper. Afterward they hurried to see how their mother was. "I guess we can't find anything that will make your father laugh," said Mrs. Disney.

"He never laughs anymore," said Walt. "He used to laugh when I rode the hogs."

"So he did!" said Mrs. Disney. "But there is one thing certain. I don't think we are very good magicians."

"I guess not."

"Our magic had no effect on him at all."

ACTING AGAIN

MAGIC SHOWS weren't the only kind of shows that Walt liked to attend. He never missed a chance to go to vaudeville shows. He also loved moving pictures and attended as often as possible.

In 1914 people began to talk about a new moving picture actor named Charlie Chaplin. Walt went to every Charlie Chaplin show that he could. Then he came home and pretended he was the actor himself.

"He's the funniest actor I've ever seen," Walt explained to his mother and Ruth.

"What does he do that's so especially funny?" asked Mrs. Disney.

"Well, the funny part comes from the way he looks. And I'll have to show you how he acts. Wait until I put on my costume."

"Oh, so you even have a costume?"

"Well, if I'm going to try out in an amateur show, I have to look the part."

Walt left the room to put on his costume, and Mrs. Disney shook her head. "That Walter! I wonder what he will think of next."

In just a little while Walt came back into the room. "How do you like it?" he asked.

Did they like it! Mrs. Disney and Ruth whooped with laughter. They thought Walt was the funniest sight they had ever seen. They were sure no one else would look as funny as he did at the amateur show. He would be sure to win.

He had borrowed a pair of his father's old shoes. They were much too big. The pants he wore were also big and baggy. Then he had added his Lincoln frock coat.

With this, Walt wore a moustache the size of a toothbrush and a little derby hat. In his hand he carried a cane whittled from a tree limb.

"Oh, Walter, come here and let me take a look at you," said Mrs. Disney.

Walt wiggled his nose and twitched his moustache. Then he began to shuffle toward his mother. As if that weren't enough, he pretended to trip over a chair. Solemnly he turned around, bowed to the chair, and tipped his hat. Mrs. Disney and Ruth laughed until they cried.

Mrs. Disney wiped her eyes with her apron. "Oh, Walter, if the real Charlie Chaplin is half as funny as you are, no wonder people like him. I would like to see him act."

"Then it's all right if I enter the amateur contest?" Walt wasn't at all sure his parents would allow him to act on the stage.

"Of course, and I just hope you win first prize. I know you deserve it."

NEW ACTS

After that, Walt not only went to the shows. He also entered every amateur contest that he could. Sometimes he won a prize. Sometimes he didn't. Walt was so stage-struck, however, that it didn't matter. He loved every minute of the time he spent watching or taking part in shows, whether he won or not.

Walt's best friend was just as stage-struck. His name was Walter Pfeiffer. Together the two boys began to work up an act. They decided to call themselves "The Two Walts."

For weeks, every spare moment they had, they spent on their act. They collected jokes, they worked out gags, and they rehearsed, hour after hour.

All this worried Mr. Disney. "I don't like it, Flora. Walt should have other interests. We don't want him growing up to be an actor."

"Oh, Elias, stop worrying. It's just a fad with Walter. He'll soon get over it."

But Walt didn't get over it. Neither did his friend, Walt Pfeiffer.

One skit the boys had worked out was very successful. They were asked to do it again and again. It was called "Fun in a Photograph Gallery."

"I can see why people like your skit," said Mrs. Disney. "That camera you boys have rigged up is the funniest I have ever seen. You both have a talent for making people laugh."

"I like the part where you squeeze the bulb," said Ruth, "and then water squirts all over the person who is posing for the picture. You always get a laugh with that part of the act."

"That was Walt's idea," said Walt Pfeiffer. "He always has lots of good ideas."

Ruth turned to Walt Pfeiffer. "I'll bet the idea for the bird flying out of the camera was yours. That's funny too."

Walt Pfeiffer nodded. "Yes, I thought up that one. We keep trying to improve the act."

Mrs. Disney smiled. "Nobody has to guess whose idea it was to draw the comic picture."

Ruth interrupted. "And then pull it out of the back of the camera, show it to the audience, and cry, 'It looks just like him, doesn't it?'"

"That's our Walter's idea. Who else's could it be? Who else could draw those pictures?"

"You're right," said Walt Pfeiffer. "And every body loves those comic pictures."

Walt said quietly, "It gives me a chance to keep in practice with my cartooning, too. I don't want to forget that."

THE JELLY FACTORY

EARLY IN 1917, the Disneys prepared to move again. Mr. Disney had become interested in a new business, a jelly factory in Chicago.

He promptly sold his newspaper route at a much higher price than he had paid for it. Then he invested his money in the jelly factory. He also invested Walt's newspaper earnings in the factory without consulting Walt.

"You'll be working in the factory," Mr. Disney explained. "You'll take more interest in your work when you have money invested.

Someday you may become owner of the factory. Then you will have a fine career ahead of you."

Walt said nothing. He had learned not to argue with his father. But he knew one thing for certain. He had no desire to be the owner of a jelly factory. He had no intention of working there longer than he had to.

"I think Walter should remain in Kansas City until school is out," said Mrs. Disney.

"You're right, Flora. It's lucky for us that Herbert now lives in Kansas City. I've arranged with Herbert and his young wife to move into our house. They'll stay until it is sold, and they've invited Walter to live with them."

"That's a good idea, Elias. Walter can also help the new owner of your paper route."

"Yes, indeed. The new owner will need help until he learns the business."

For once Walt dreaded to see school come

to an end. Of all the uninteresting work to look forward to, a jelly factory was the worst. Walt shuddered at the thought.

Herbert's heart went out to his kid brother. One day he said, "I've a suggestion for you, Walter. How would you like to be a news butcher this summer? It might be a lot more fun than working in a jelly factory."

"News butcher?"

"Yes, that's a job riding on trains. You'd walk through the trains and sell things to the passengers. You'd sell things like soda pop, sandwiches, candy, and magazines."

"Oh, I'd like that. I'd earn some money and get a chance to see the country at the same time. How do I get the job?"

"I'd suggest you try the Van Noyes Interstate News Office," Herbert told him. "I hear they're looking for a boy for summer work."

As usual, Walt wasted no time. His lively interest and his experience in working impressed the men at the news office. They were soon convinced that he should have the job.

Walt left the office floating on air. He loved trains. He had loved them ever since his first long ride from Chicago to Marceline. Now he'd be riding trains every day. He'd see Oklahoma, St. Louis, Chicago, Jefferson City—places he hadn't dreamed of seeing this summer. Walt's heart jumped with joy.

Walt's first day on the job was an eight-hour run from Kansas City to Jefferson City, Missouri. It was a hot, muggy day, and he was sure he could sell all the cold drinks.

He began hawking his wares at the rear of the train. "Cold drinks! Sandwiches! Candy! Magazines! Newspapers!" he called loudly. "Does anybody want a cold drink?"

"Here, I'll take one," said a young man.

"Me, too," said another.

"Don't forget us over here," said a lady with some children. He sold six drinks there before he went on to the next seat.

Walt opened pop bottles right and left until his supply was gone. "I'll be right back, folks," he said. "I'll just have to go up front and get some soda pop."

But when Walt came back he had a surprise. The last two coaches were no longer on the train. "What happened to those coaches?" Walt asked the conductor. "All my bottles of pop were on them. Everybody wants cold drinks."

"Oh, my!" said the conductor. "That's too bad. Didn't you know? Those two coaches were only going as far as Lee's Summit."

The worst of it was that Walt had to pay for all the empty bottles he lost. Therefore, his first trip was not a financial success. He never made such a mistake again. After that, he knew exactly where every car was going.

The railroad crews soon began to know Walt. They liked him and helped him in every way they could. Walt didn't forget them, either. He made sure he had cold drinks or sandwiches or whatever else they liked whenever they wanted them. In exchange, an engineer now and then would let Walt ride up front in the engine for part of the trip. Some people might have objected to the heat and the cinders. But the more Walt knew about trains, the better he liked them.

Walt couldn't have been happier. Even the mishaps that took away his profits failed to discourage him. One day he picked up a beautiful basket of fruit that he was supposed to sell. "I'll make a profit this trip," Walt thought. "Nobody

will be able to resist apples and bananas and pears like these."

Walt was right. People bought the different kinds of fruit in a hurry. But as the fruit disappeared, Walt noticed a funny odor and saw an unusual number of fruit flies. He soon found that every piece of fruit beneath the top layers was rotten. He could not sell it.

"That's a rotten trick to play on a news butcher," said the conductor. "You make little enough at best. You're not the first one to get cheated, either. But we can't keep that stuff on the train. I'm sorry you won't have a chance to return it. People will complain about the smell. We'll have flies. We'll have to throw it off. There's nothing else we can do."

Walt's biggest problem, however, was himself. Never before did he have a chance at so much candy and soda pop. He ate and he drank, but of course he had to pay for it. The trips were long, and he had a healthy appetite. When he got to the end of a trip, he almost always found he had eaten all the profits.

In two months Walt's job as news butcher came to an end. Walt didn't have a cent of profit to show for his long hours of work. But he had a lot of happy memories. He also had a love for trains that would never leave him.

CHICAGO

In Chicago, Walt attended McKinley High School. He contributed art work to his school paper, *The Voice.* Three nights a week he attended the Chicago Academy of Fine Arts.

When he wasn't in school, he worked at the jelly factory. He prepared the fruit for the jelly. He ran the machinery, and he helped with the packing. Once he served as night watchman when the regular watchman was ill. In this neighborhood burglars often broke into the factories. He was rather frightened at the idea of going through the factory alone at night, but he was determined that no one should know it.

When school ended the following summer, Walt began to look for other jobs. One job he found was that of gateman on the Wilson Avenue Elevated Railway. He also worked at the post office, where he delivered mail, picked up mail, and helped out with the general deliveries.

With all this to keep him busy, Walt should have been satisfied. But he wasn't. The United States had been at war in Europe for more than a year. Troops were leaving every day to fight in France. On every side people were urged to buy Liberty Loan Bonds. Brass bands played. Patriotic songs were sung. One of the most popular songs was called "Over There."

Roy had joined the navy. Another brother was in the army. For some time Walt had been trying to figure out a way he could go over there, too. The trouble was that nobody wanted a boy unless he was eighteen years old. Walt was still only sixteen, and he felt useless.

"Shucks! The war will be finished before I get a chance to find out what it's all about," Walt thought sadly.

Another boy at the post office had the same problem. One day he said to Walt, "Say, I've found a way for us to get to France."

"Oh, Russ, that's wonderful. What did you find out?" asked Walt eagerly.

"We can join the American Red Cross. They need ambulance drivers, and they'll take you if you're seventeen years old. We'll get to France and be right on the front lines if we carry wounded soldiers off the battlefield."

"That's fine, Russ," Walt said sadly, "but I'm not even seventeen yet."

"Well, neither am I," Russ answered. "But you said you got your job here at the post office by making yourself up to look older. Why can't we try the same trick at the Red Cross?"

"Sure we can. I like that idea. I can easily fix us up to look older than we are."

Walt's makeup worked splendidly. The boys were accepted. Just when they were rejoicing they ran into another problem. It was all right if they were only seventeen years old, but their parents still had to sign their passports.

Walt took his passport application home and asked his parents to sign it. However, he had known before he asked what the answer would be. "No," said Mr. Disney. "I'll not be a party to signing your death warrant."

"Elias, he's determined to go, whether we let

him or not," said Mrs. Disney. "If we don't sign it, he'll find another way. Don't you think we might as well give our consent?"

"Very well, Flora. If you want to sign it, go ahead. You can sign for me, too. But I won't be a party to it."

For a minute Walt was overjoyed. Then he saw something that made his heart sink. His mother had written his birthdate as December 5, 1901, and he was afraid she wouldn't change it.

"Mother, that shows I'm only sixteen years old. Can't you make it 1900?"

"No, Walter, I can't," she declared. "You were born in 1901, not 1900."

"I know, but they'll never take me unless I'm seventeen years old. They think I look seventeen. They said so."

"Oh, all right, Walter. I suppose it won't hurt. You really will be seventeen in just a few months. But I won't change it myself. If you want to change it, go ahead."

Mrs. Disney turned her back while Walt carefully changed the "one" to a "zero." Now at last he was a member of the American Red Cross. He hoped he'd soon be on the way to France.

For a time Walt's unit stayed in Chicago, where the members lived in tents. These young men had to be trained before they could be sent overseas. Walt had to learn to repair motors.

As if a world war were not enough trouble, a great flu epidemic spread over the nation in 1918. Soon the hospitals were overflowing with patients. Many doctors and nurses were ill, and there was not enough help to care for the sick.

At that time there were few medicines to combat the disease, and many people died.

As members of Walt's unit began to get the flu

and were taken to the hospital, Walt hoped he would not get sick. He wanted to get to France as soon as possible. However, before long, he was seriously ill. Since he lived in Chicago, he was taken home to be nursed back to health by his mother. While he was ill, his unit was transferred. Walt was assigned to another unit, which trained in South Beach, Connecticut.

"OVER THERE"

On November 11, 1918, Walt's unit was still in South Beach, Connecticut, awaiting shipment overseas. Then word came that the armistice had been signed. Everybody there was glad the war was over, and yet they were sad. They were sure they would never get to France now.

But a few nights later there was loud shouting in the barracks. "Everybody up! Everybody up! Everybody up!"

"What's the matter?" cried the young men. "Has the war started all over again?"

"Fifty of you fellows are going to France."

Walt had almost given up hope of being chosen as name after name was read from the list. But the fiftieth name called was his. Within a few hours he was on a ship, sailing to France. Although the fifty men traveled on an old cattle boat, Walt enjoyed every minute of the trip. At last he was having a real adventure.

In France there was still plenty of work to do. Walt drove supply trucks. He drove ambulances. He served in the canteen.

One day Walt said, "Why don't we put up some posters. Then when the troop trains stop, the boys will know we've got hot chocolate and doughnuts and showerbaths."

"That's an excellent idea," said the Red Cross director. "But we have no posters."

"I can make some. I like to draw," said Walt. "I'll start right now."

After that everybody began to find out about Walt's drawing. He made posters. He drew pictures on his ambulance. He painted a Croix de Guerre on the back of his leather jacket. He decorated his footlocker.

"Say, how about painting my leather jacket?" asked one of the boys.

"Mine, too," said another.

Soon Walt had a prosperous business. Everybody wanted his jacket and footlocker painted. One young man had the idea that Walt might decorate German war helmets and make them look old. The two boys went into business together. Walt did the decorating. The other boy sold the souvenirs to the troops as they passed on their way home. The two did a thriving business.

Walt stayed in France almost a year. His life wasn't always easy. At times he was bitterly cold. Sometimes he was hungry. Other times he had nowhere to sleep except on a hard floor. Often, if he had a bed, it was full of bedbugs.

But Walt felt just as he did when his news butcher job came to an end. He had loved the whole experience.

Unlike his news butcher job, this time Walt had made a profit. Altogether he had sent home five hundred dollars for his mother to keep.

★
HOME FROM FRANCE

WALT CAME home from France loaded with gifts for his family. It was good to be back in Chicago with his mother and father and Ruth. But the happy reunion lasted only a short time.

Almost at once Mr. Disney spoke of the jelly factory. "Walter, there's a job waiting for you at the jelly factory. It pays twenty-five dollars a week. The manager tells me you'll have a good chance to go higher, too."

Walt shook his head. "Thanks, Dad. But I've thought about it a great deal lately. I've made up my mind. I'm going to be a cartoonist."

"Now, Walter, listen to me. While you were in school, I went along with your foolish ideas of becoming an artist. But now you're seventeen years old. It's time for you to give up such foolishness and get down to work."

Walt stood his ground. "I'm sorry to disappoint you, Dad," he said firmly. "I've always wanted to be an artist. I know I wouldn't ever be happy doing anything else."

"You'll starve, Walter," Mr. Disney warned. "You'll never be able to make a living."

"Well, I'm going to try," Walt declared. "I've made some sample drawings, and I'm planning to go to Kansas City to look for a job."

BACK TO KANSAS CITY

Walt looked forward to getting back to Kansas City. Roy was there. So was Aunt Maggie. As soon as he arrived Walt began his search for a job. For a while he had little luck.

Then one morning Walt stopped in the bank where Roy worked. A friend of Roy's said, "I know where you might get a job. I heard the other day that the Gray Advertising Company is looking for an artist for the Christmas season."

Walt lost no time in calling on the company. He showed them his sample drawings. The office manager studied Walt's drawings carefully. Then he asked, "When can you start to work?"

"Right away."

"The job will pay only fifty dollars a month. Will that be all right?"

"Will it!" Walt almost shouted with happiness. Later he chuckled to himself. "That's only half as much as the jelly factory would pay me, but I don't care. At last I'm going to work as an artist. Aunt Maggie will be glad to hear that, even if Dad isn't. Mother will, too."

Walt hurried to tell his aunt the news. Aunt Maggie was surprised when she saw Walt. He had changed a great deal in the years that he had been away from Kansas City. He was not quite eighteen years old, but he was a handsome, husky young man now, with big hands and big shoulders. His aunt hardly recognized him.

"Oh, Walter, how you've grown!" cried Aunt Maggie. "How glad I am you came to see me."

Walt gave his aunt a big hug. She had changed, too. Walt was surprised at how frail and tired she looked. "I had to come, Aunt Maggie. I have some wonderful news. Of course you are the person had to tell first."

"Oh, Walter, tell me. What is it?"

"I'm an artist at last, Aunt Maggie. I've got a job. Just imagine! They're going to pay me fifty dollars a month for drawing pictures."

"Walter, that's the happiest news I've heard for a long time. As you can see, I've been ill. I haven't heard much good news lately."

His aunt was indeed ill. Walt could tell it was an effort for her to be the gay, happy Aunt Maggie of his childhood.

"Is there anything I can do?"

"No, no, Walter. Your visit has been the best medicine I could have."

"Do you remember the time you came to our farm and brought me my first drawing tablet?"

"I certainly do. You had just drawn a picture of your pig on the side of the house." For a moment Aunt Maggie's eyes sparkled in the way Walt remembered. "I'm glad to see you still have the same eagerness for being an artist."

"I owe a lot to you, Aunt Maggie. You were the first one who took my drawing seriously and gave me the encouragement I needed."

Aunt Maggie smiled wanly. Walt knew she was very tired by now, so he kissed her and said good-bye. He left the house feeling sad. He was sorry that he had reached his goal too late for Aunt Maggie to enjoy his triumph.

NEW WORK

Walt's job at the Gray Advertising Company lasted for six weeks. Walt worked hard, and he kept his eyes and ears open to learn everything he could. He learned many things, practical things that every artist should know.

Walt also made a new friend, another young artist named Ub Iwerks. When the Christmas business rush was over, both boys were laid off.

Ub was upset at being out of a job, but Walt

was not worried. "Let's start our own business," Walt suggested.

"That's fine with me," said Ub. "But how do we start with no money and no equipment?"

Walt was full of ideas and enthusiasm. "First I'll see if some company will give us desk space in their office. In exchange, we'll offer to do their artwork. Then we'll have no rent to pay. I'll send home to Chicago for my five hundred dollars to buy our equipment."

"Hey, wait a minute. That sounds great, Walt. But what I can do?"

"Well, you're better at lettering than I am, Ub. You've had more experience in doing other kinds of artwork, too."

"Thanks, Walt."

"I'll go out and drum up business. You can take care of the inside work."

"You can count on me."

Walt grinned. "Of course, I want to help with the artwork as much as I can. I've got to keep in practice."

The boys found desk space in an office in the Railroad Exchange Building. Only one thing bothered Walt. Their names were listed on the billboard in the lobby as "Disney-Iwerks." Walt didn't like this.

"Sounds like we make glasses for people with bad eyes," Walt worried. "We'd better change it to 'Iwerks-Disney, Commercial Artists.'"

"However you want it, Walt," said Ub. "But your name deserves to be first. This business was your idea. It's your money that has paid for our equipment."

"It makes me feel proud either way. Every time I look at our names on the billboard my chest swells up. I almost burst the buttons off my coat. Not many people have their own business at our ages. Don't you feel proud, Ub?"

"Of course I do, but I can't express myself as well as you can. You feel things. You're able to make other people feel them too. That's a wonderful gift you have, Walt."

The new business got off to a splendid start. The first month the boys made one hundred and thirty-five dollars.

Then one morning before long Ub called Walt's attention to a newspaper advertisement. The Kansas City Film Ad Company needed a cartoonist. Walt read the ad with interest.

"It's exactly the kind of work you've been wanting, Walt," Ub urged. "You'd be working with films and cartoons together."

"It's too good to pass up," said Walt. "I'll go talk with them. If they like me, maybe they'll let me keep our business, too."

The ad company liked Walt all right. "But

we want your full attention on your job. There can be no business on the side," said the boss. Walt talked to Ub about the problem.

"I'll take over the business," Ub promised. "And I'll repay you out of my profits for the money you spent on our equipment."

Two months later Ub came to Walt. "The business is no good without you, Walt. I've lost everything. Is there any chance of my getting a job at the ad company too?"

"You're a fine artist, Ub. The company would be foolish if they didn't give you a job. I'll speak to the boss about you."

Walt went at once to his boss and told him what a talented artist Ub was. "If you recommend him, Walt, that's good enough for me," said the boss. "Tell the young man to come to work. We can use him."

Soon Walt and Ub were working together

again. They both liked everything they did, but most of all they were enchanted with the animated cartoons. These cartoons were made with little paper cutout figures. Their paper legs and arms worked on dowels. In this way they could be moved into any position the artists desired as they were being photographed.

Walt and Ub studied these cartoons day and night. They read every book in the library on the subject. They talked about animated cartoons and ways to improve them all the time.

One day Walt said to the boss, "Why don't we make the drawings on celluloid and then photograph them one above the other?"

"Yes, I suppose they could be done that way," replied the boss. "But I think we'll stick to the way we're doing it. There's nothing wrong with the method we're using now."

"Of course there isn't," said Walt. "But I'd

still like to do a little experimenting with my idea. Would you mind if I borrowed the camera some night and worked it out at home?"

Walt had to ask several times before the boss agreed to the use of his camera. But since the boss liked Walt, he finally said yes.

Walt's night work began to pay off. First he made some animated cartoon advertisements that were one minute long. He called them Laugh-O-Grams and sold them to a chain of local theaters.

Next Walt decided to animate some fairy tales. These were to be seven minutes long. But for these Walt needed help. "If there were only more hours in the day!" Walt sighed. But he was still working all day at the Film Ad Company, and his nights were taken up with his Laugh-O-Grams. There was no time left for him to draw the cartoons for the fairy tales.

"I know what I'll do," Walt decided. "I'll run an ad in the newspaper. I'll find some young artists, and I'll offer to teach them how to animate cartoons in exchange for their help."

Walt's idea worked fine. A couple of boys

replied to his ad, and the fairy tales were put into production. When seven of them were done, Walt hired a salesman to take his fairy tale cartoons to New York City.

By this time several people had become interested in Walt's work. They were willing to invest their money in a small company that Walt decided to form. He called it the Laugh-O-Gram Corporation. Now Walt gave up his ad company job and became president of the new company. His career as an artist was indeed doing well, and Walt was not yet twenty-one.

For a while things couldn't have been rosier. Then suddenly Walt's distributors in New York went broke. So did Walt's business.

Walt racked his brain for ideas to save his company. He even tried using people with cartoon characters in a film which he called *Alice in Cartoonland.* But nothing helped. Walt's business went bankrupt, and he was back where he started. He didn't have a penny.

One day the restaurant where Walt had been eating stopped his credit. For two days Walt lived on canned beans and stale bread.

"Gosh, I wouldn't want Dad to find out about this," thought Walt. "He always said I'd starve to death. Now he'd be sure he was right."

Luckily the restaurant owner had a change of heart. He finally told Walt to go ahead and eat. "Your credit will be good for as long as you need it," he said. "I know you always pay your bills when you have any money."

Walt no longer had a bed to sleep in. In fact, he no longer had a room. Instead, he slept in a chair in his studio.

His only companions were the mice that played in his waste basket. One little mouse was especially friendly. Walt called it Mortimer.

Sometimes Mortimer sat on Walt's drawing board, watching him as he worked.

One afternoon a friend called Walt to come over and see him immediately. He wanted to talk about Walt doing an animated cartoon.

Walt said, "I'd be delighted to come, but I haven't any shoes to wear."

"You haven't any shoes? Why not?"

"Well, my only pair of shoes is at the repair shop. The repair man won't let me have them until I pay a dollar and a half, and I'm broke."

"I'll fix that," said his friend. The friend came over at once and got Walt's shoes out of the repair shop for him.

One day Walt had a chance to borrow a motion picture camera. Walt loved cameras almost as much as he did cartoon work.

"I know what I'll do," Walt decided. "People always take great pride in their children. I'll see if I can make a little money taking motion pictures of babies."

Walt went from house to house knocking on doors and taking pictures. Soon he had earned enough money to buy the camera. Then he sold the camera at a profit. Altogether he had enough money to buy a railroad ticket to Hollywood, California, with forty dollars left over.

Walt had a couple of reasons for wanting to go to California. The center of the motion picture industry was in Hollywood, California, and Walt had never gotten over being stage-struck. He still had a desire to work in motion pictures. Besides that, Roy was in California. He had been there for some time. He was in a veterans' hospital recovering from tuberculosis.

One day in July, 1923, Walt fed Mortimer an extra ration of cheese. Then he took the mouse to a field where it could find a new home. Walt stroked the mouse's furry head tenderly. "Good-bye, Mortimer," he said.

Then Walt hurried to the railroad station to get aboard the train for California. His pants were threadbare. His coat didn't match. His suitcase was cardboard. But Walt had only one idea. He'd go to Hollywood. He'd be with Roy, and he'd get a job in motion pictures. What's more, he was determined to be a success.

WALT CREATES A MOUSE

WALT ARRIVED in Hollywood with big ideas. He had decided to find a job as a movie director. For days he tramped from one motion picture studio to another with no luck.

After a while he changed his mind. He'd take any kind of job so long as it was in a motion picture studio. He said he'd even take a janitor's job if there was nothing better. Still he had no luck in finding work.

Finally Walt was so penniless that he went back to his cartoons. First, he made joke reels and sold them. Then he began his *Alice in Cartoonland* series again. This time he not only used a live Alice, but he used other children and a dog from the neighborhood.

Roy was out of the hospital now. The brothers rented one end of a real estate office to use for their studio.

One day Walt said, "I guess it's best that you take care of our money, Roy. I can draw cartoons, but I'm not very good at managing money."

Roy agreed. From that time on Roy was in charge of their finances. Often money was so scarce that they barely had enough for food. Sometimes when they went into a restaurant, Roy would have to remind his brother, "You order a meat dish today. I'll get a vegetable. Then we'll split the orders. That way we'll both have a balanced meal."

After a while, with Roy's careful management,

things improved. Both boys decided they could afford to get married.

Walt had a staff of artists working for him now. Among them was his good friend, Ub Iwerks. The *Alice in Cartoonland* series had been replaced by an *Oswald the Rabbit* cartoon series. Oswald was doing extremely well. His contract would soon come up for renewal, and Walt decided to ask for more money.

"I need more money if I'm going to expand our business," Walt told Roy. "I have several new ideas I want to try out too."

One day in 1927 Walt and his wife, Lilly, set out for New York. There Walt talked to Oswald's distributor. Instead of more money, however, the distributor offered Walt less money. When Walt refused, he said, "It makes no difference whether you sign or not. I have your best artists signed up to work for me. We can make *Oswald the Rabbit* without you."

"I created Oswald. He's mine," said Walt. "You can't do me this way."

"Oh, can't I?" said the distributor. "Take a close look at your contract, Disney. You don't own Oswald at all."

Walt studied the contract carefully. It was true. He and Roy had not read the fine print as well as they should have.

For a moment Walt reeled from the blow. Then he rushed back to his hotel. "Come on, Lilly," he said to his wife. "Let's pack right now and catch the next train for California. I have to think of an idea for a new cartoon series. What's more, I have to get home as soon as possible and hire some new artists."

On the train Walt thought and thought. Somewhere after crossing the Mississippi River, Walt cried, "I have an idea, Lilly. Mortimer

Mouse! How does that sound?"

"It sounds awful," said Lilly. "The mouse is all right, but the name sounds silly to me. Can't you think of a better name?"

"Well, we'll change it to Mickey Mouse," Walt said. "How do you like that?"

"I like it much better."

"Good," said Walt. "Then my new series will be about Mickey Mouse. We'll make Mickey Mouse better known than Oswald the Rabbit."

Making animated cartoons was not easy. Walt was using almost the same process he had developed in Kansas City. But just to make Mickey move once on the screen required sixteen drawings. For a ten-minute cartoon, 14,400 pictures had to be drawn. This called for a lot of patience, a lot of time, and a lot of money.

Walt's old friend, Ub Iwerks, had remained loyal to Walt. Now he and Walt worked like

beavers until they had two films on Mickey Mouse completed. They called them *Plane Crazy* and *Gallopin' Gaucho*. A third one was almost ready. "It's going to be the best one yet," Walt said, as they checked what they had done.

Then new trouble came. Up to this time, motion pictures had been silent. Now, all of a sudden, a way had been discovered to make talking motion pictures. People rushed to see pictures with sound, but they were no longer interested in going to see old-fashioned films.

"We'll have to make our cartoons talk too if we want Mickey to be a success," Walt told Roy. Roy groaned. Then he started to think how he could raise money for expenses.

Walt went to work to figure out a score for his third Mouse film, which he called *Steamboat Willie*. There was very little sound equipment available, and Walt had none at all. So he took his film to New York to have the sound recorded.

Many film companies were recording sound on phonograph discs to play at the same time as the picture. This was easier and cheaper, but Walt didn't like that method. He insisted the sound must be on the film itself.

"Suppose the film and the record are separated and one or the other is lost," he argued. "Or suppose the record and the film don't run at exactly the same speed. Then they won't come out together. It's too big a risk."

Back in Hollywood, Roy was doing his best to keep Walt supplied with the money he needed. Soon their funds were all used up. Roy finally had to sell Walt's car to make ends meet.

Walt had marked his film carefully so that the music and sound would be exactly right with the film. Nevertheless the orchestra Walt hired had a terrible time.

Several times the bull fiddle with its heavy sound blew out tubes in the recording machine. The orchestra went over the score again and again, but it couldn't keep in time with the film. Walt worried as he saw the recording costs skyrocketing. He tried to tell the orchestra leader what to do, but the man ignored him.

Walt took the part of Mickey's voice. He also took the parrot's part. When the parrot yelled, "Man overboard!" Walt coughed. Then he looked about sheepishly. He knew what he'd done. He had blown out a tube himself. At last, however, everybody did his part right. *Steamboat Willie* turned out to be a big success.

Soon the whole world began to know and love Mickey Mouse. Madame Tussaud put Mickey in her famous wax works in London, England. The Encyclopedia Britannica devoted a separate article to him. Mussolini adored Mickey. Adolf Hitler hated him. Queen Mary of England loved him. So did President Franklin Roosevelt.

Mickey's picture on their products saved several toy manufacturers from going broke. The League of Nations endorsed Mickey as a "symbol of international good will." The Academy of Motion Picture Arts and Sciences gave Walt a special Oscar for creating Mickey.

Walt didn't stop with creating Mickey Mouse. He began to create other cartoon characters like Donald Duck, Pluto, and Goofy. Also, just as Walt had insisted on putting sound on his films, now he insisted on making another change. This time he decided to add color.

Roy and Walt argued about this. In the end Walt won the argument. Roy agreed to look around for ways to raise more money. One of Walt's earliest color successes was *The Three*

Little Pigs. This proved Walt's imagination could produce something besides the Mouse.

One day in Paris, France, Walt went into a movie theater that advertised a Mickey Mouse film. But instead of one Mickey Mouse film, several were shown, one right after the other. Now Walt had another idea. Why not make a full-length cartoon film? He decided to do *Snow White and the Seven Dwarfs.* This took two years, for he was working on other projects too.

Among these projects was a film called *The Old Mill.* In this cartoon he used a technique that was more complicated than any he had used before. Up to this time film cartoons had looked flat. In *The Old Mill* Walt added three dimensions, or a feeling of depth, to film cartoons. This short cartoon was practice for the techniques to be used in *Snow White,* but Walt won an Academy Award for *The Old Mill.*

As usual, Roy had to worry about raising money for Walt to go ahead with his work in making *Snow White.* Although they had known the new process would be expensive, this was costing far more than they had anticipated. One day, in the middle of the film, Roy said, "Walt, we'll have to let the bankers see what we're doing if we're going to get any more money."

Sadly Walt agreed, but it was against his principles to let outsiders see his unfinished work. One Saturday morning the bankers, Roy, and Walt gathered in the projection room. Walt showed *Snow White* as far as it had gone. He explained the parts to come if he had the money.

The bankers remained silent except for an occasional "Uh-huh." Walt thought, "Gosh, this is terrible. They don't like it at all. We won't get the money to finish it."

The bankers continued to remain thoughtful as Roy and Walt walked them to their car. Walt opened the door of the car and held out his hand. One of the bankers shook it thoughtfully. "Walt," he said, "you've got a gold mine in that picture. It will make you a lot of money."

Walt breathed a sigh of relief. "Hurrah!" he thought. "We've won." They had, too. *Snow White and the Seven Dwarfs* became one of the top money earners of all time. It also won for Walt a big gold Oscar and seven little Oscars, one for each of the Dwarfs, from the Academy of Motion Picture Arts and Sciences.

WORLD WAR II

Suddenly the world was at war again. When the United States entered World War II, the army took over Walt's studio at once. It was a very good place from which to guard the airplane factories in California.

Early in the war the army, the navy, and the air force came to Walt for help in preparing training films. The Treasury Department asked for a film to persuade people that it was patriotic to pay their taxes. The Department of Agriculture wanted a short cartoon to show how food could win the war.

They all knew people would watch Walt's cartoon films and learn from them. It would be much more difficult and take twice as long to teach these things with dull lectures.

Foreign governments came to Walt too. Navy and airmen asked Walt to design insignia for their ships and planes. It was a busy time for Walt. He gave fully of his rich imagination to all of them.

During the early days of the war there was

already talk of the day when the Allies would join forces and regain the territory they had lost to the enemy. As the military leaders planned and schemed, they knew there was one thing they must have. It was a code word that would be familiar to all of them, no matter what their language or their nationality.

On June 6, 1944, the Allied invasion of France began. The code word chosen for the entire operation was "Mickey Mouse."

After the war was over, Walt spent several summers in England. There he tried his hand at making live-action films from the old legends and stories that he loved. The lovely English countryside made a perfect setting for stories like *Robin Hood*, *Treasure Island*, *The Sword and the Rose*, and *Rob Roy*.

Back in the United States Walt began to make nature films. In working with the animals for his cartoons, Walt had never liked to study them in cages. Several times he had sent out photographers to photograph the animals in the wild.

It was soon found that the camera could find and tell the secrets of nature that man could never see with his naked eye. The camera could travel places that most people would never have a chance to go. This led to some of the most beautiful nature films ever made. Walt's imagination seemed endless.

★

THE MAGIC KINGDOM

NOBODY KNEW exactly when the idea for Disneyland started. Not even Walt himself knew. But sometime through the years the idea was planted in his imagination, and it grew and grew.

The idea could have had its beginning the day Walt made his first long train ride from Chicago to Marceline. Many a night afterward Walt lay awake waiting for the engine to come whistling across the prairie. He loved the sound of that train whistle!

He was never more proud than when he rode the train as news butcher. Once in a while the engineer would say, "Come on, kid. Ride up front and keep me company." Walt never forgot the joy of touching the throttle.

One day many years later, Walter said to his wife, "I've always wished I could have a train of my own someday. Now think I've found a way to have one. I can build a miniature railroad around our house."

"Well, I suppose it's all right, Walt," said his wife, Lilly, "so long as you don't tear up my flower beds."

"Oh, I won't hurt the yard," said Walt. "I can tunnel under your flower beds if I have to."

"The birds and other animals around here eat all the strawberries and peaches and other fruit we grow, now," Mrs. Disney continued. "I don't want my flowers ruined too."

"You can get all the fruit we need at the market, Lilly," Walt reminded her. "But all the wildlife would have to go somewhere else to live if we didn't have a food supply for them. We'd miss the animals a lot more than we'd miss a few strawberries and grapes."

As usual, Walt went to work right away. First, he studied the slope of the yard. Then he designed the layout for the tracks. He had a tunnel dug under Mrs. Disney's flower beds, just as he had promised. The tunnel was reinforced with steel and concrete, so that it couldn't cave in and destroy the plants. A year later Walt had his track completed.

He had also built a perfect miniature coal-burning locomotive, similar to the ones he had loved when he was a boy. The locomotive was scaled an inch and a half to a foot, with enough cars to seat a dozen people.

After that, when guests came to the Disney home, Walt would ask, "How would you like to have a ride on my train?" Of course the guests always wanted to take the ride. So Walt would put on his engineer's cap and his overalls. He'd tie a red bandanna around his throat and carry an oilcan like a real engineer. Walt had a passion for making everything as authentic as possible.

Then he'd fire up the engine, and away they would go. The guests squealed with laughter. Walt, too, never failed to have the time of his life on these rides.

The idea for Disneyland more than likely had its start when Walt was a boy. He never missed a chance to go to the carnivals and amusement parks of Kansas City. He was still fascinated by this type of entertainment.

Later Walt had two little girls of his own named Diane and Sharon. He liked nothing better than to take them to the parks and the zoos in California. While the little girls enjoyed the rides, Walt would sit on a park bench eating peanuts. That's when he first began to think about having his own park.

"It would be nice if a park offered something that was fun for fathers, too," Walt thought.

When the Disneys built their new studio in Burbank, California, Walt made a suggestion. "Why don't we take a couple of acres and make an amusement park here by the studio?"

Poor, long-suffering Roy knew whose job it would be to raise the money for such a project. He turned a deaf ear to Walt.

Walt continued, "We can't have visitors running all over the studio. But when they are nice enough to call on us, we could let them visit our park. Our employees and their families would enjoy it, too."

Roy still said nothing. He hoped his silence would persuade Walt to give up the idea. Roy should have known better. Walt continued to mull over his idea. At every chance he visited parks, fairs, and zoos. When he was in Europe he went to the Tivoli Gardens in Copenhagen. When he was in New York, he stopped at Coney Island. He wrote to other amusement park owners. He began to draw up plans.

Walt also quietly borrowed money on his life insurance and looked around for a place to build his park. He found it in a 165-acre orange grove in Anaheim, California.

One day Walt took Roy out to Anaheim to show him what he had in mind. "We'll call it Disneyland," said Walt. "It will be a Magic Kingdom where everybody, young and old, has fun. We'll divide our little kingdom into four major lands," Walt continued. "We'll call them

Adventureland, Frontierland, Fantasyland, and Tomorrowland. We'll tie them all together with a pretty little street lined with old-fashioned shops. We'll call it Main Street, USA. Now, how do you like that, Roy?"

"Well, of course I like it," said Roy. "I generally like your ideas. Since you've lured me out here, tell me more."

"Well, we'll have a miniature railroad with a track that runs all around our Magic Kingdom," Walt went on. "In the center of our kingdom will be Sleeping Beauty's Castle. That will be the symbol of Disneyland.

"At the entrance to our Magic Kingdom we'll have a town square with a city hall, a fire station, and an opera house. There will be horse-drawn streetcars and an omnibus on Main Street. We'll have band concerts and parades down Main Street too.

"In Adventureland we'll have a tree house, and we'll have a jungle cruise. There will be crocodiles and elephants and hippopotamuses. But, of course they won't be real."

"Wait a minute, Walt," said Roy. "There's no water here. How can you have a cruise?"

"Don't you see, Roy? That's the beauty of this land. It's nice and flat. We can change it any way we wish to suit ourselves. We can make our own hills and mountains and rivers and lakes just the way we want them.

"In Frontierland I'm going to have a river with a Mississippi steamboat. I'll call my boat the *Mark Twain*. In the center of the river there will be Tom Sawyer Island. You'll reach that by a log raft."

Roy groaned. Walt ignored his brother's groans and went on talking. "When you cross the drawbridge into Sleeping Beauty's Castle, you'll be in Fantasyland. There we'll have all our little characters meet people—Mickey Mouse, Dopey, Grumpy, Jiminy Cricket, Pluto, Goofy, Donald Duck, and the Three Little Pigs. Even Big Bad Wolf will be there. Do you get the idea? Do you know what I mean, Roy?"

Roy nodded. "I know what you mean, Walt. It will cost a fortune."

Walt's eyes were shining. By now he didn't even notice Roy's groans. "We'll have a King Arthur carousel, not just a plain old merry-go-round. The horses will be the prancing steeds of King Arthur's knights. We'll have flying elephants like our Dumbo. And there'll be a tiny Storybookland where people can see Cinderella's castle, the homes of the Three Little Pigs, and Pinocchio's Village. At night, we'll have fireworks over Sleeping Beauty's Castle."

"I'm almost afraid to ask," said Roy. "What's

Tomorrowland going to be like?"

"I'm coming to that. There we'll have a monorail, a rocket flight to the moon, a submarine voyage. Those are just a few of the things I have in mind. We'll get the help of our country's leading scientists for Tomorrowland. We'll want everything to be authentic."

"Walt, do you have any idea how we'll raise the money for all this?"

"Well, I've been hinting to our good friends at the Bank of America," Walt said. "I think they like the idea."

"You mean you've already talked to them?"

"Oh, yes. And another way I can get people interested in our park is through television. The television people have been after me for some time to do a TV show."

"That's true," Roy agreed. "A tie-in with Disneyland sounds great."

"Then you'll go along with me, Roy?"

Roy smiled. "Don't I always go along with you, Walt? I'll get busy and see what I can do about raising the money."

"I knew you'd see it my way, Roy. You always do." Then Walt teased, "Though sometimes you're a little stubborn." Roy grinned. Each brother understood the other. They both knew Roy's down-to-earth management was just as important as Walt's imagination.

On July 17, 1955, Walt's dream came true. Disneyland opened, but Walt considered opening day only the beginning. "Disneyland will never be completed," he said. "It will continue to grow as long as there is imagination in the world." Disneyland has been growing ever since.

One of Walt's favorite attractions, which has been added since 1955, is called "Great Moments with Mr. Lincoln." This noted attraction seems to make Abraham Lincoln come to life and to speak. It reflects Walt's attempts as a boy in school to make the great president come alive for his listeners. This attraction is made possible by Audio-Animatronics, a process developed by Walt and his staff.

Kings, queens, prime ministers, and presidents have visited Disneyland. Many, many more people have come who had no claim to fame at all. They are all welcome—young, old, rich, poor, famous, and unknown. Here for a few magic hours they can throw off their worries and cares. They can do almost anything they ever dreamed of doing if they use a little imagination.

Walt's Disneyland has been called one of the wonders of the modern world. Walt Disney has been called the most significant figure in the creative arts since Leonardo da Vinci.

HONORS TO WALT DISNEY

In Walt Disney's office there is a case filled with more than nine hundred honors bestowed upon him—medals, statuettes, plaques, and golden cups. In 1964, President Lyndon B. Johnson awarded Walt the Presidential Medal of Freedom, the highest decoration the United States government can bestow upon a civilian.

Though Walt never graduated from high school, his old school at Marceline, Missouri, gave him an honorary high school diploma. Five colleges gave him honorary degrees.

Of course all these honors brought happiness to Walt. But he was not concerned so much with being honored as he was with the challenge of creating the impossible.

Walt left one dream to be fulfilled. That was a dream of a school of creative arts to be known as the California Institute of the Arts. This would be a school where people interested in any of the creative arts could study. Here they could learn to give the world the full measure of their talent and imagination, just as Walt Disney had done in his busy life.